MEDIEVAL MURDERS

Medieval Murders is a prequel to the Ray Elkins mystery series. If you are a reader of the series, you know that the first four books are set in Cedar County, an amalgam of the many lakes, forests, and towns found in northwest lower Michigan. In these books there are references to Ray's earlier professional life, when he taught criminal justice at a large Midwestern state university. The plot in *Medieval Murders* revolves around the deaths of three members of the English department. It's a younger Ray Elkins, more hair, fewer pounds, but still very grounded.

MEDIEVAL MURDERS

AARON STANDER

WRITERS & EDITORS
INTERLOCHEN, MICHIGAN

Publisher's Cataloging in Publication Data
Stander, Aaron.
Medieval Murders / Aaron Stander. – Interlochen, Mich.: Writers & Editors, 2011.

ISBN: 978-0-9785732-6-3
1. Murder–Michigan–Fiction. 2. Murder–Investigation–Fiction.

Printed and bound in the United States of America
Cover and interior design by heatherleeshaw.blogspot.com
Cover photograph Mark Smith

FOR BEACHWALKER,
WHO HELPS THIS ALL HAPPEN.

MEDIEVAL MURDERS

1

〜〜〜

Shortly after 8:00 A.M. on the last Monday in August, Alice Wid-dowson, secretary to the chair of the English department, arranged the handouts for the first and longest faculty meeting of the academ-ic year. She had tables set up on each side of the central entrance to the auditorium in Old West Foundation Hall, the building occupied by the department. On the right, in alphabetical order, were folders for the regular faculty; the ones for the adjuncts were on the left. Widdowson—trim, mid-fifties, with a military bearing and an aura of authority, reading glasses on thin gold chains hanging against a carefully pressed white blouse—acknowledged each arriving fac-ulty member in a manner appropriate to their rank and station.

The department early birds picked up their materials, greeted col-leagues, and after finding seats, looked through the bundle of Xerox copies, each topic identified by paper color. The majority came in a few minutes before nine, reached over one another to get their pack-ets, and stood around talking until Widdowson, using both arms in a shooing motion, herded them into the lecture hall. Some settled into seats, others wandered around the room, shaking hands and chatting. The stragglers—three tenured faculty members, all male, sauntered in shortly after nine. By that time Widdowson had moved all the materials to the right hand table. In each case she peered at her watch as she handed the latecomer their materials. Finally, when only one folder remained, Widdowson got up and closed the doors to the auditorium.

At five minutes after the hour, Professor Clifford Chesterton, the department chair, in an impeccably tailored three-piece blue suit, entered the auditorium from a side door and mounted the lectern. He switched on the light and carefully arranged his notes. The glare reflected off the typed pages onto his gold-rimmed glasses. Several shushes finally brought the audience's attention.

In a ministerial chant worthy of a High-Church Anglican—sans incense and bells—Chesterton launched into his opening remarks. He reviewed how enrollment patterns were affecting curriculum, credit hour production, staffing, and tenure considerations. Between each major point he paused dramatically and looked at his audience, a spotlight clearly illuminating his large face and meticulously coifed steel-gray hair. It wasn't so much what Chesterton was saying that caused the anxiety for many in the audience, it was the subtext of his remarks, an underlying theme that shaped careers, tenure, and the personal and professional lives of many in the room. He didn't have to say 21 sections of Women's Literature and nine sections of African-American Literature and five of Hispanic Literature made it this term, but only three sections of Shakespeare. Everyone knew the numbers. And he didn't have to tell the congregation that the only section of Milton was canceled because of low enrollment. They knew the trends. They'd been logging into the system and watching enrollment in the department.

Chesterton was the man in the middle. The new university chancellor and the cadre of corporate managers he surrounded himself with were demanding that the academic departments become "customer oriented" and "user sensitive" and that class schedules and course offerings be constructed in response to "market forces" and "consumer demands." Increasingly, the department's funding was based on body count, the total credit hours produced. He did his best to protect his colleagues and the integrity of the department and the discipline, hoping that this current administrative fad, like all others he had witnessed over the years, would pass without doing too much damage.

The last topic Chesterton broached, the only one that aroused the interest of the somnolent audience, was a detailed analysis of the tenure prospects of department members. He reviewed funding trends in the university and explained how those were tied to enrollment patterns. He quoted members of the academic episcopacy—deans, provosts, vice-chancellors, and the chancellor—on the university's financial condition. There was little good news, especially for the untenured.

As was the custom at the opening faculty meeting of the school year, Chesterton introduced the newest members of the department, six women and one man, all fresh from graduate school with newly minted Ph.Ds.

Then the Directors of Undergraduate Studies and Graduate Studies, two men almost Chesterton's age, each provided commentaries on the current enrollment numbers, the data appearing on a screen behind them in PowerPoint charts and graphs. Finally, Alice Widdowson cautioned the faculty to be parsimonious in their use of office supplies, especially when it came to the Xerox machine.

A few minutes before the hour, Chesterton closed the meeting, his arms raised in a benediction-like gesture, with a reminder that he and his wife would be hosting the annual fall cocktail party on Saturday evening at their home.

The carillon was just striking ten as members of the department flooded onto the sidewalk in front of Old West. When questioned after the event, a few thought they saw something fall. Many heard the dull thud as an object crashed onto the large rectangle of gray granite pavers that surrounded the base of the carillon. All remembered the horror they felt when they realized what the object was.

An academic robe, luxurious folds of heavy black silk and rich blue velvet, covered the bird-like figure. A soft velvet hat with gold braid lay next to the crushed skull. Small streams of blood drained from the mouth and nose, forming a pool around the tassel.

Alice Widdowson took command. She ordered everyone away from the body and directed someone to call the University Police. Some members of the department rushed away, appalled by the ghastly scene. Others moved in to get a better view. Only Chesterton approached the body, kneeling at the side for a long moment, extending a hand as if to palpate the neck for a pulse, then pulling it back without touching the crumpled form. Rising slowly, he carefully surveyed the scene, and then walked away, the silent crowd separating, allowing him to pass through.

Widdowson stood guard until the first officers arrived and cordoned off the perimeter of the carillon. Then she went back into Old West and made a fresh pot of Earl Grey tea.

2

~~~~~~

When the clock radio, tuned to the university station, had switched on shortly before 6:00 A.M., Ray Elkins was finally in a deep sleep. For several minutes he had been able to merge the Vivaldi into his dream, but when the announcer started to read the news, he groped for the switch. He slid back into a troubled sleep for a few minutes, and then willed himself awake.

It had been a long night. Exhausted, he had dropped into bed shortly before eleven and immediately slipped into a dreamless slumber, but within two hours the old demons were working upon him. He followed his usual pattern, wandering through the dark house, using the toilet, drinking some water, returning to bed, and drifting off again. He had repeated this pattern several more times.

Elkins had always been a light sleeper, at least in his adult years. But this new pattern, this napping between nocturnal wanderings, had started in the course of his long-term companion's illness and had continued on since her death, more than a year before.

During Ellen's last months he would wake, listen to her breathing, and wonder about the future. His despair had started long before she was gone.

His inability to sleep was one of the problems discussed by his death and grieving group at the medical center. The group leader, a psychiatrist, said "sleeplessness and sleep interruptions were com-

mon after a loss, and these problems lasted for months, and sometimes for years."

Elkins climbed out of bed and pulled the sheets and then the blankets in place, straightening the pillows. After showering and shav-
ing, he went to the closet to get his clothes.

The two halves of the walk-in closet were a mirror image of each
other, the same hanging space, the same arrangement of shelves,
drawers, and cubicles. One side was empty. The other was crowded
and in disarray, but Elkins had never been able to cross the line, to
overflow into what had been her space.

Ellen's mother and sister had stayed on a few days after the funeral to help dispose of her things and put the house in order. Elkins, while wanting to be helpful had avoided the process, spending
most of his time at the office, making unsuccessful attempts to lose
himself in work. When he returned home in the evening, he was
impressed with how much the two women had accomplished. They
had organized her clothing: sorting, washing, and folding. Usable
clothing had been delivered to a local women's shelter. The rest,
placed in plastic trash bags, formed a neat row along one side of the
garage.

He knew that they were also grieving, but they channeled their
energy to do what needed to be done, and their efforts, while not
relieving the sorrow, gave them a sense of purpose. He wondered
about the differences between men and women, speculating that
women might be better able to cope with the big things, things like
birth and death. But then he questioned if this was only his inability
to accept Ellen's death, a fact that had nothing to do with gender
differences.

Well before 8:00 A.M. Elkins was working at his desk. His tenure as acting director of the university police would be ending in
five days, and he was determined to have all the current paperwork
completed before Friday.

He had been pressured by Chancellor Pearson to leave his post
as chair of the criminal justice program and fill this interim position with the university police. Pearson had assured him that it was
a short-term assignment. Elkins was to restore discipline and rees-
tablish administrative control over the scandal-ridden department

while the university conducted a national search for a new chief administrator. The assignment provided a new focus in his life, and he was able to get rid of much of his gloominess by burying himself in work. But as September approached, he was glad that the end was in sight and he would soon be able to return to a more academic view of law enforcement.

He had close to two hours of paper work completed when the phone interrupted him.

"Sir, Johnson in Dispatch. We've just had a report on a probable suicide. Thought you'd want to know. Someone has apparently jumped from the carillon. Lieutenant Pascoe is on her way, and I've notified EMS and called the coroner."

"The carillon? How did someone get in there?"

"I'm sorry, sir. I have no other information."

"Thank you. I'm on the way."

Elkins grabbed his sport coat off the hook and went down the back staircase to the rear exit of the University Police Center, a substantial two-story brick structure erected in a drab 30s style at what had once been the far edge of the campus. For several decades it served as the university's College of Agriculture before they moved to a new satellite campus several miles south of town.

The director's car, a bulbous black Crown Victoria, the vehicle favored by police departments and the retired, was baking in its designated place a few feet from the back entrance. As he opened the door, he was hit by a wave of hot, stagnant air. Windows open and air-conditioning on full, he drove toward central campus.

The destination was less than a mile, but his progress was slowed by the heavy traffic. The streets surrounding campus, adjacent to the dorms, Greek houses, and apartments were jammed with the vehicles of returning students. As he waited for the congestion to clear, he observed the carnival-like atmosphere as the college kids, some with parents, unloaded cars, vans, and small trucks.

There was so much vitality in the scene, the excitement of a new year, and the promise of new challenges, future careers, friendships and romances. As Ray watched he thought that death is not common in the valley of the young, not common because youth is usually free from the ravages of disease that accumulate with age. And yet they're not immune; binge drinking, accidents, suicides, and drug overdoses could take a tragic toll.

Elkins drove around the barriers to the service road that ran to the rear of the carillon and parked at the end of a line of emergency vehicles. He walked toward the circle of police and EMTs.

Charlene Pascoe, Head of Investigations, met him half-way and walked with him toward the carillon. The gray granite obelisk stood at the center of a small block, surrounded by sidewalks in an "X" configuration from each corner. Triangular lawns, some with extensive flower-beds, filled the spaces between the pavement. The east side of the carillon faced the west perimeter of central campus, some of the buildings dating back to the origins of the school. The university's auditorium, named after a railroad tycoon who gifted much of his fortune to the school, stood on the west side. On the north was the School of Graduate Studies, a mixture of classical and gothic styles, constructed in the 1920s. And on the south, the School of Architecture, a 50s-modern design, in thin tan brick and aluminum, the masonry now bearing dark stains from the metal oxide.

A decade before Charlene Pascoe had been one of Elkins's most promising undergraduates, and a few years later she had returned to campus to get an M.S. in Public Administration. She was the first of three division heads he recruited as he rebuilt the department's command structure. Char had been working in one of Chicago's affluent north shore communities. There she had been quickly promoted from day-to-day police work to liaison officer, a position where an articulate, bright young woman helped the department's image on a variety of fronts. At first she had been flattered by her rapid advancement, but events quickly forced her to confront her own naiveté. Her feelings about her position, combined with the ending of a relationship, made Elkins's job offer, although it was less remunerative, especially appealing.

"What do we have?" Elkins asked, brushing up against her shoulder.

"The victim jumped or fell from the carillon," she said, lifting the yellow plastic ribbon for him to duck under.

When they got to the body, Elkins dropped to his knees and gently pulled back the blanket. A shudder ran through his frame as he confronted the contorted body and smell of death. He pulled the blanket over the corpse.

"Not pretty," said Char.

"Did you ever work homicide in...?" he asked after a long moment.

"Only at the edges. Never a permanent assignment."

He stood and looked at her. "Get pictures, measurements, and check for any other physical evidence. I'd like a diagram of the scene. Have you checked the carillon?"

"Door's locked, and it's an off-master key. Maintenance is bringing one."

Elkins looked at the side of the carillon, moving away from the tall stone structure to get a better perspective.

"Had to fall from there," Pascoe pointed to a small window near the top of the tower.

"Any idea of...."

"That woman, the one in the green, Widdowson's her name, she says the victim is Sheila Bensen, an English prof.

"Witnesses?"

"Yes and no," said Char. "The English department's meeting had just ended, and they were leaving West Foundation. Several say they saw something fall or heard the impact." She handed Elkins an open note-pad. "I've got their names and addresses. None of them saw her climb out of the window. They just saw movement."

"Anyone see her enter the building?"

"We haven't found anyone who...."

"Did someone see her this morning, before the meeting?"

"No one I talked to."

"Find out where she lives, who saw her last. Just good spade work. Here's our guy with the key." He motioned in the direction of a man being allowed to duck under the yellow plastic tape. "Hi, John," said Elkins.

"Oh, my God," the man said as he looked toward the blanket.

Elkins gently grabbed him at the elbow and moved him toward the door. "What's the deal with this lock? General master won't open it."

"It's one of the oldest on campus. They're supposed to work with the new master, but this one's cranky. I imagine you'll be needing this key for awhile."

Elkins nodded.

"Keep it as long as you want."

"John, how many people have a key for this building?"

"I can't say for sure. Professor Pennington has some. He keeps losing them. He gives them to students, and he doesn't get them all back. When the maintenance guys need access to the building, they usually come for one when their masters don't work. Most times they return them, but not always."

"And the general master doesn't work."

"Some do, some don't. It's the person as much as the key, you get what I'm saying. Too much in a hurry. They don't feel the mechanics of the thing, just jam it in and expect it to open." He slid the key into the lock, jiggled it, turned it counterclockwise, and pushed open the door. He withdrew the key and handed it to Elkins. "Send it back when you're done." They stood and watched John hurry away.

"Well, now we know how secure things are," said Pascoe . They entered and stood in the cool interior, allowing their eyes to adjust to the dim light.

Then Elkins found the light switch. "Ever been in here before?"

"Once, years ago, during freshman orientation."

A worn oriental rug covered much of the interior floor. Dull blue slate tiles ran from under the rug to the rectangular blocks of stone that formed the walls. A steel stairway, three feet wide, ran along the sides of the building, with a small landing at each level as the staircase made 90° turns. They ascended the steps, taking pains not to use the railings, their footsteps echoing, breathing hard as they reached the top floor. The large baton keyboard for the carillon stood at the center of the small square room on a worn and dusty hardwood floor. Ray noted how much the keyboard resembled a piano. His eyes followed the steel cables that ran from the back of the keyboard to a mechanical maze of turnbuckles, tumblers, clappers, return springs, and dozens of bells overhead.

"So she used the chair to climb up. The window is not very big," said Pascoe, calling his attention to the east window, one of four windows, five feet above the floor that looked out over campus, the metal sash pushed to the right. A chair stood below.

"Yes," said Elkins, inspecting the window-frame. "There was no room for her to sit and ponder whether or not she wanted to go through with this. All she could do was pull herself through the window and tumble."

"I can't imagine," said Pascoe with a shiver. "The mate's on the ground next to the body," she said, pointing to a small black shoe.

"See if you can find evidence of the shoes on the chair or if she used them to help push herself up the wall." Elkins pointed to the dull gray granite. "Dust the door handle, railings, chair, sill, window latch, anything she might have touched. Look for fibers, especially near the chair and around the window. And the key, look for the key."

Elkins moved toward the stairs. "And call Dr. Gutiérez in pathology at Medical Center and brief her. When the M.E. has signed off, get the body over there. I'd like the autopsy a.s.a.p. I'll adjust my calendar so I can attend."

As Elkins drove across campus, he thought about the changes in his professional life in the last six months. For more than a dozen years his focus had been teaching and writing about criminal justice, and in the last few years he had become an academic department chair. The sudden temporary assignment of running the day-to-day operations of a campus police department had been a dramatic change.

Looking at the body really hit him. Perhaps it was Ellen's death. Death had become so real. Or maybe, he speculated, he had been away from real police work so long that he had lost his ability to be a disinterested observer.

3

~~~

Elkins paced the outside perimeter of the emergency entrance of the University Medical Center, a large new facility centered on a mile-square campus, just beyond the urban sprawl. Two years before, rows of corn rose on the flat terrain. Now the area was covered by concrete and monolithic structures of reflective glass, stainless steel, and granite.

Twenty minutes after the agreed upon time, red faced and breathing hard, Clifford Chesterton came marching up the drive.

"Sorry I'm late," he said. "It was hard to get away. Things are in absolute chaos in the office. A few days ago no one had a kind word for Sheila. Now they're hysterical over her death."

"I'm sorry I have to ask you to do this. We've checked with Human Resources. She doesn't have any family locally. In fact, it doesn't appear that she has any living relatives."

"She lost a mother or father after she got here," said Chesterton. "I'm not sure which. Back East somewhere. I never heard her talk about anyone else."

"The body, especially the head and face, was damaged quite severely in the fall, and I...."

"Elkins, you don't have to prepare me. My father was the chief pathologist at Rush Presbyterian in Chicago for over thirty years. I've seen a lot of bodies."

Elkins guided Chesterton to the morgue. They were met by an attendant who led them into a locked room. The body, covered by a sheet, was on a gurney. Ray pulled it back to expose the head.

"That's Sheila."

"You're sure."

"Of course I'm sure," Chesterton responded, crimson rushing to his cheeks. "I had to deal with this woman for seven years. This is the body of Sheila Bensen."

Elkins covered the body and led him out into the hall, "Do you have time for a cup of coffee? I'd appreciate it if you could tell me about her."

Chesterton nodded. Ray had known him for years. They were neighbors, both served on the faculty senate and the department chairs' council. Ellen and Chesterton's wife had been close friends.

"We are talking about suicide, aren't we," Chesterton asked as he stirred his coffee.

"It looks that way, but we have to rule out the possibility of homicide. Tell me about her."

"Sheila," he paused, his large face glistening with perspiration, "Sheila was a very complex, difficult person." He slowly added a second bag of sugar and stirred the coffee again. "This would have been Sheila's eighth year at the university. She did not attain tenure. As you know, normally her seventh year would have been her last, but since her appeals dragged on until the end of spring term, the provost granted her an additional year of employment. I think Keith was covering his ass, giving the appearance that the university had gone way beyond what it was obligated to do. He anticipated further litigation."

"Why wasn't she tenured?"

"Several reasons, actually. First and foremost, she didn't publish. Well, that's not quite accurate. She had one short article that summarized her dissertation work, but that was her first year. She's done absolutely nothing of a scholarly nature since then. It's the expectation of the department that junior faculty members publish a number of articles and at least one book before they come up for tenure." Chesterton paused and looked into Elkins's eyes. "The woman was incredibly productive, but she didn't put her energy in the right place if she wanted tenure."

"I don't follow," said Elkins.

"She worked on feminist issues and did a good deal of writing related to those causes, but it wasn't scholarly writing. When she submitted her portfolio for review, she had volumes of published materials, but none of it—except that one article I mentioned—was in a juried journal. During her tenure fight—she did every level: department, college, university, and finally the board of governors— Sheila contended that her writing was at the vanguard of humanistic studies, that stuffy old journals weren't ready for her work. And at every level, people tried to point out to her that these publications weren't in her field, medieval literature. Indeed, they weren't even in her discipline and didn't conform to any of the basic tenets of scholarship."

"How did she respond?"

"You couldn't talk to Sheila. She believed what she wanted to believe." Chesterton paused and looked thoughtful. "I also think part of the problem was her supporters."

"How so?"

"Most were undergraduates. They don't understand the issues. They supported her out of personal loyalty and believed that the whole tenure thing was the university's attempt to get her for her feminist activities. It all got quite irrational. Elkins, you must remember some of this. The *Daily* had an article or an editorial on Bensen's tenure problems almost every day during the winter term." Chesterton stopped, looked across the table, and read Elkins's lack of response. "Well, maybe not. You were occupied with other things then." He paused and started again in an attempt to change the subject, "I imagine you're glad to be finished with this assignment."

"Yes. Friday's my last official day. I've said I'd be available as necessary for a week or two to help the new person settle in. I'll be so damn glad to have this done and get back to my old life."

"What's your fall schedule like?"

"I'm teaching a seminar and chairing a couple of dissertations, the usual administrative duties." Changing his tone, he said, "Getting back to Bensen, is there anything else you can tell me?"

"I've explained the tenure issue and publication. That was only part of the problem. Her teaching wasn't particularly good, either. I had a lot of complaints. You're a department chair; you know the problem. When students seek you out to bitch about a professor, you can almost guess who it will be. I have sixty-five full-time people; ninety-five percent of the complaints are about four people. Sheila was one of the four."

"What kind of things?"

"The usual. She didn't show up for class, wasn't prepared, didn't return papers, was sarcastic and condescending, couldn't or wouldn't explain why she had assigned a certain grade. I don't know how many times I talked to her about these problems."

"And her response?"

"She blew me off, said she didn't have time for the 'carping little bastards,' her words. She said teaching got in the way of her real work."

"Which was?"

"Her various causes. She was sort of a cult leader, Sheila and her sophomore groupies. I've heard that Sheila wasn't well liked by the main-line women's groups. She always needed to be in control. There's one more thing about the tenure issue."

What's that?"

"Sheila was a medievalist. We have five medievalists in the department. One is tenured, four are not. Actually, we don't need five, two would be enough, but when Keith was chair, before he moved over to Provost, he was enamored with the idea of building a big graduate program, a center for English literary studies on the great American prairie, or something of the sort. He hired lots people with specialties we didn't need. Of the four untenured members, Sheila had the poorest record of publication and service to the department, and, as I've told you, her teaching was dreadful. She's not the kind of person we would ever tenure."

"The other medievalists, where are they in the tenure process?" Elkins asked.

"Two come up this year and one the year after next."

"And you will only tenure one of them?"

"Probably, depending on a retirement. Our undergraduate enrollment continues to fall, and our graduate numbers are depressing. At this point it's hard to convince the university that we need any additional tenured faculty."

"Sheila, did she act depressed? Would you have suspected that she might kill herself?"

"No. But you have to admit, this was very dramatic, wasn't it? Waiting for the meeting to be over and then splattering herself on the pavement in front of her colleagues, the people she held accountable for not supporting her. And in her academic robes, that's a nice bit of cheek. That was Sheila. She was a master at inflicting guilt—right up to the end."

"Did she have friends in the department?"

"Not men friends, she was hostile toward men."

"What are you suggesting?" asked Elkins.

"I'm not suggesting anything. I'm making a statement. She was openly hostile to men. I think from her political perspective, we are responsible for most of the things that are wrong with the world. She was a very unpleasant, angry woman, a real piece of work."

Elkins was about to pursue Chesterton's last remark when he was interrupted by the beeping of his cell phone. He fished around in his coat pockets for the phone and then looked at the number. "That's the chancellor's office. I imagine Pearson wants to see me immediately."

"I bet he does," Chesterton agreed. "He doesn't like anything that brings reporters around, and this certainly will.

One more thing…"

"What's that?"

"Stephanie and I are having our annual fall party for the department on Saturday night. I know Stephanie hopes you'll be there. Can I tell her you're coming?"

"Thanks, I'll have to see." Elkins's tone changed. "If you think of anything that I should know, please call me."

"You can count on it, Ray."

Walking to his car, Elkins reviewed the conversation in his mind. Then he remembered a faculty member his department had chosen not to tenure and the anguish that had followed, the lawsuit, depositions, and months of turmoil.

Elkins had left his car at the far end of the parking lot, his attempt at working some exercise into a busy day. When he reached the vehicle, he walked beyond it to the end of the pavement and looked west, across the fields of corn. A mass of dark gray clouds appeared across the horizon. He stood for several minutes and watched the storm slowly advancing. He remembered as a teenager kneeling on the hot sand on the top of the Sleeping Bear Dunes up in Michigan and peering at the wall of thunder clouds rolling across the big lake. He held onto those happy memories as he drove back toward campus.

4

Ray Elkins' first stop on Tuesday morning was the university's administration building on central campus. Sharon Anderson, secretary to the Chancellor, looked up from her computer display as Elkins entered the outer office. She stood to greet him, a warm hug ending with her taking his right hand in both of hers.

Sharon had been a friend of Ellen. In the months since Ellen's death, he had felt ill at ease in Sharon's presence. He had tried to analyze his reaction to her, but had not come up with an adequate explanation. Perhaps seeing her intensified his memories of the period before Ellen's death when Sharon and a few other close friends were constantly in the house providing help and support. He also suspected, although he didn't have one iota of evidence, that Ellen, near the end, was looking for a woman for him, and Sharon was her choice.

"He's expecting you." She withdrew her hands and gestured toward the door to the inner office.

"How is he?" asked Ray.

"He just got back from playing golf with the president of the board. He called it a working meeting," she answered with a wry smile.

"Did he stop at the nineteenth hole?"

"I imagine so, he's got that aura."

"Aura," said Ray. "Always the diplomat." He rapped on the door and waited for a response from within before entering.

John Pearson sat behind an imposing walnut desk positioned in front of a glass wall that looked over the central campus quadrangle. Ray could see the carillon directly across the quadrangle. Trees and other buildings obstructed his view of the lower half of the structure, but the top, with its east-facing window, was clearly visible.

Tall, balding, a former college football player running to fat in late middle age, Pearson got up and came around the desk, extending his hand, an enormous championship ring covering the upper half of his fourth finger. He gave Ray a firm handshake before he sank into one of the two overstuffed leather chairs in front of the desk and motioned for Ray to take the other with a commanding gesture.

"I need to talk to you about a number of things, but this Bensen woman moved you up several days on my calendar," Pearson began. "I need a damage report."

"Damage?" Elkins repeated. He glanced over Pearson's shoulder at a collection of photos. Sharon referred to it as the wall of holy relics. At the center was a large picture of the last football team to win a national championship. Pearson, the team's captain, was in the middle of the photo holding a football. At the sides and below were pictures of Pearson with political and sports luminaries.

"I just want to make sure we're clean."

"Clean?" repeated Elkins, pulling his attention back to the conversation, trying to anticipate where Pearson was going.

"You know that woman was a real pain in the ass. I want to make sure there's nothing the media can use against us. It is suicide, isn't it?"

"It appears to be. I won't have a definitive answer until the investigation is completed."

"Well, I want it done fast, then I want you in front of the cameras. That bitch was crazy as hell. Do you know how much money she's cost the school? Her and that fucking feminist lawyer of hers. Get the investigation done, Elkins. Get it done and tell the world. She was loony, and she offed herself."

Pearson pushed his rump to the left and leaned on the right side of his chair, "There are a couple of other things I need to talk to you about. First, and I'll do this again in some kind of public forum so you get the recognition you deserve, I want to thank you for accepting this interim position. We had a hell of a scandal on our hands, and we needed integrity, someone who had credibility with the faculty. Who better to do the job than the chair of the department of criminal justice and former chair of the faculty senate.

"You're a chancellor's dream, Elkins, a chancellor's dream. I cleaned house in the athletic department and got them back on track. In just a few months you've made the university police an effective, incorruptible agency again. The days of payoffs to jocks are over. And we won't have any drugs or rape in the athletic dorm with the police looking the other way. You did a good job, Elkins, fast and professional. We'll give you a plaque or something. I know you don't care about that kind of shit, but we'll do it anyway. You know what the big problem is around here?"

Elkins waited, knowing Pearson would answer his own question.

"It's all these god damn intellectuals, especially those bastards in the humanities. They don't like me because I was the president of a big steel company. I'm not one of them. And that's exactly why the Board hired me. I care about this school, and I know how to get things done. None of those pointy-heads do. I like you guys in the applied areas, you know how to make things happen." He paused and looked at Elkins.

"Thank you, I think," Ray responded.

"Now, Elkins, the next thing I got to tell you, you're not going to like. You're expecting to be out from under this interim thing by Monday."

"That was our agreement." said Ray, moving uncomfortably in his chair.

"Well, I'm afraid we're going to have to modify the agreement. This isn't public yet, but your replacement, Don Thompson, called late Friday afternoon and turned down the job. We've got a contract with the SOB's signature on it, but how the hell are we going to hold him to it?"

"What happened?" asked Ray.

"His wife. Says she refuses to come, refuses to bring the kids. I don't know if that's the truth or not. If it is true, we're damn lucky we didn't get him. Any man that can't stand up to his wife sure can't be trusted to manage a major department. Anyway, that's why I was meeting with Bradford earlier today, needed to inform the Board. We'll have to repost the position and form a new screening committee. It will probably take most of the fall semester. Bradford and I both think that it would be in the best interest of the university if you would stay on as interim. What do you say?"

Elkins looked out the window, across to the carillon. "It creates a lot of problems. I'm teaching a seminar, and I've got graduate students that...."

"We need you to do this. Why don't you approach it this way: get someone to teach your seminar. If you want to, go ahead with your graduate students. I'll get you a supplemental contract for that work. But continue on in this position. I promise I will have a replacement before the beginning of the winter term. What do you say?"

"Do I have much of a choice?"

"Fuck, yes, you got a choice, free country and all that," said Pearson. "But I know you're a team player. You'll do the right thing for the university." He pointed at Ray's chest with his index finger to emphasize this point. "There's one more thing I need to tell you. Bradford wants you to know that the board is going to endow a chair in the music school in memory of Ellen."

Ray felt the blood rush to his face as the anger throbbed through his body. "Were you planning to tell me this before or after you had my decision?"

"Suspicious bastard," Pearson retorted with a chuckle. "This has been in the works for awhile. You know how slowly things get done around this university. And I meant to tell you before. I just never had the opportunity. Ellen, how long has she been gone now?"

"More than a year," Ray answered.

"Are you seeing anyone?" Pearson probed.

"Seeing?"

"A woman, Elkins. You need a woman. When my first wife died, I was lost for a while, but fortunately someone new came into my life. You've got to get on with living, Elkins."

Ray again moved uncomfortably in his chair. He needed to get out of there. Pearson didn't notice. Changing the subject he continued, "Elkins, get me that report as quickly as possible. We'll have university elations organize a news conference to put the proper spin on the facts. I want a nice, clean suicide. You know what I mean, no complications." He stood again and firmly held Ray's hand for a long moment as he repeated, "A nice, clean suicide with no complications."

On the way out, Ray stopped at the side of Sharon's desk.

"How did it go?" she asked.

He moved his head from side to side, unable to find the right words.

Sharon looked at him, a smile spread across her face, and she began to chuckle. "That bad, huh?"

"Yes," he answered, her warmth breaking through his tension.

"This too, shall pass." She paused briefly. "You should come to my yoga class. You need a little more Zen about you."

"Zen," Ray repeated, looking back at her before he left the office.

As he waited for the elevator, facing the wall of marble and stainless steel, in the empty hallway, he was angry with himself, sorry that he hadn't told Pearson to stuff the job.

5

~~~~~~~

Char Pascoe was waiting at Elkins's office when he returned from his meeting with the chancellor. She had carefully laid out neat piles of materials on the conference table.

"What do you have?" he asked.

"Here are the photos. The first set is with the body. The second with chalk outline. I'll scan these into the computer and put the measurements in for you. I also have some prints. Didn't find any usable prints on the door or knob on the first floor or around the window. We went over everything very carefully. We did get a good set off the chair by the window. I'll check for a match with Bensen's. We found something else that you'll be interested in."

"What's that?"

"On the floor under one of the pedals of the carillon keyboard," she paused and pulled a plastic bag from her portfolio, "we found this key. Don't know how it got there, like maybe she tossed it. I've checked. It's the key to the entrance door. There are partials on the key. I'll see if these are Bensen's prints."Pascoe continued, "Here's a copy of her complete HR file. I thought you might want to look at that." She placed the file in front of Elkins.

"Do you have anything else? How about her office?"

"I'm scheduled to interview her office-mate, a Barbara Castlemain, in a few minutes. Do you want to come?"

"Sure," he answered. "You can drive."

Elkins held the door open and followed Pascoe into the building. Old West Foundation Hall was almost deserted in the late afternoon. The hot air smelled of dust, old wood, and varnish. They climbed the stairs to the second floor and followed the numbers to 231. The door stood open. Elkins gazed into the large office. A fluorescent fixture, one of the four tubes flickering, hung from the twelve-foot ceiling. Sunlight from a large window cut obliquely across the room.

Barbara Castlemain rose from her chair and came to the door to greet them. A sleeveless, blue cotton dress, carefully pressed, covered her tall, slender frame. Wisps of gray showed in a tight bun, and a pair of gold half-lens glasses rested on her aquiline nose.

"Hello, Ms. Pascoe, and this is...."

"Ray Elkins, the acting head of...."

"Oh yes, Professor Elkins," she brightened a bit, giving him a weak smile and extended a limp hand. "I've seen you at Faculty Senate meetings." She motioned toward two empty chairs. "I'm sure I don't have anything more to tell you," she offered, looking at Elkins.

"We have a few questions," he began.

"It was suicide, wasn't it?" Castlemain asked.

"All unnatural deaths have to be thoroughly investigated. It's standard procedure. And we need to gather some additional information." Ray could see her discomfort. Was it just an aversion to talking to the police or was there something she didn't want to tell? He glanced around the office. The right half of the office, Bensen's side, was in chaos—the desk piled with papers, shelves heaped with books and stacked with more papers, the floor covered with overflowing cardboard boxes, additional heaps of papers, and two plants, shriveled and long dead, on the window sill. The left side was a study in organization and order, a desktop with only a phone and calendar, books aligned at the edge of shelves, and a small refrigerator with a microwave on top. "Perhaps we should start with how long you knew Sheila Bensen," said Ray.

"Seven years. We shared an office since her first semester." Castlemain stopped, focused first on Pascoe, then on Elkins. "What kind of information are you seeking?"

"Anything that you think might be helpful." Pascoe paused. "Were you surprised by her death? Was there any indication that she might be suicidal?"

"Before I answer the question, let me talk about the nature of our relationship. Sheila and I weren't close. Yes, we shared an office, but I didn't know her very well. We weren't friends, we were barely colleagues, and we didn't do anything socially. She was difficult and very unpleasant. I don't know about the suicide. Sheila was rather bizarre, but I don't think she was a depressive. That wasn't part of her craziness."

"Would you tell us about her, to use your term, craziness?" asked Elkins.

"I think much of it had to do with the tenure issue. Well, that's not completely true, but let me start there because I think it all fits together. Sheila was an angry person, and after she didn't get tenure, her anger intensified. She felt people in the department were out to get her."

"How do you know?" Elkins watched her eyes, watched the small wrinkles increase as she processed his question.

"Well, it's not that she said much to me, she probably thought I was in the enemy camp." There was a long pause, and then she continued. "I guess most of it I overheard, phone conversations. And it's not that I was trying to...."

"Who was she talking to?"

"I'm not sure."

"Her lawyer?"

"No, I don't think so. Remember, I was the enemy. She played to several audiences." She glanced at Pascoe, then focused on Elkins.

"Audiences?"

"Yes. Different tones, different messages. When she was talking to one of her supporters, her followers, she could be quite inflammatory. She'd say lots of wild things, and her language was, well, rather crude. When she was talking to people who I think were her personal friends, she used a different tone, and the conversations seemed much more rational."

"Let me go back to an earlier comment. You said she felt people were out to get her, and you suggested that this was an inaccurate perception. Did she have enemies in the department?"

"She didn't have any friends in the department, but I don't think she had real enemies, either. Her problems here were professional, and you know how tenure works," she looked directly at Elkins. "Jobs are scarce, tenure's hard to get. If you're untenured, every time someone gets it, your chances diminish, or at least that's how some people look at it. But Sheila's reactions were a lot more para-noid. She hadn't done any of the required things. She didn't publish, and she refused to serve on department committees. The criterion for tenure is very specific. Sheila went out of her way not to meet it and then attacked us for not tenuring her. It's like she wanted to fail. Does that make any sense?"

"It's illogically logical. I think we all know people who do that," responded Elkins. "Can you speculate on why she...."

"Well, I'm not one for amateur psychiatry, but I think her whole personality turned on being an outsider. She needed something to push against."

"You said she played to two audiences. Would you elaborate on that?" asked Pascoe.

"Her first audience was young women, undergraduates for the most part, members of various feminist groups. You know the kind, long on rhetoric, short on action. The protest is more important than fixing the problem. It's probably exciting and romantic to be out there pointing out what's wrong with the world, especially when you never have to get your hands dirty working out the solutions. But that was Sheila, all theatre. A real Jean Brodie with her girls. That's what makes the suicide rather surprising."

"I'm not following," Elkins gave her a questioning look.

"I'm surprised she didn't get some of her followers to take the plunge. It would be more like Sheila to stand on the side and lecture on the meaning of their sacrifice." She stopped, and Elkins noted that she looked embarrassed.

"And the other audience?" he probed.

"Given what I overheard, I think the people were either in other departments or from the community. Like her psychiatrist, she was always calling and changing or canceling appointments."

"Do you know the name of the doctor?"

"The name is Margrave, that's his last, don't know his first name. And she did a lot of things with the Catholic Church on campus. She often called Father Bob. I assume he's the priest there. I could never quite understand that whole thing."

"Why?" asked Elkins.

"She was always going on about how the Catholic Church was the embodiment of paternalism and the greatest oppressor of women in the world, and yet, by all appearances, she was a fairly devout Catholic. But then there were lots of things I didn't understand about Sheila. She described herself as a radical vegetarian and animal rights advocate, but every week or two I'd find her eating a Coney dog she had smuggled in. I once confronted her on it, and she told me she really liked Coney dogs, said it was her one inconsistency. I didn't bother to mention a few others."

"Do you know anything about her family?"

"Her mother died a few years ago. I think her father was long dead. She never said anything about siblings, so I always assumed that she didn't have any, although I don't know that for sure."

"Do you know of any romantic interests?" asked Pascoe.

"Well, no. I didn't see her in the company of any men, and they didn't come around here looking for her. Other than Margrave and Father Bob, I didn't hear her calling a specific man on a regular basis." She paused. "I do know she took part in some gay rights activities, but I never knew if her participation was anything more than an act of solidarity."

"You did manage to get along?"

"Yes, it's interesting. We worked out a relationship of sorts, a live-let-live arrangement. Sheila had her own way of organizing," she gestured to the other side of the office, "and I have mine." She paused and looked thoughtful. "I have to tell you that even though I found her rather difficult, there were some good things. She was a poor teacher. She didn't do enough preparation and was completely disorganized, but she cared about some of her students. I watched her counsel them, work with them. She could be very kind. Do you know what I'm saying? There were many inconsistencies in her character. It's hard to say who she really was. There were times I liked and respected her. There were other times when I was ambivalent."

"Do you know if she ever received any threatening letters or phone calls?" Elkins asked.

"I don't know about phone calls or letters. I do know, boy do I know, that she had some pro-life people unhappy with her. Remember two years ago when that group came to town and tried to close the Family Planning Center?"

Elkins nodded.

"Sheila organized the opposition. She made sure that there were enough 'choice' people—students, faculty, and townspeople—that the crazies were outnumbered and out-shouted. During that time our office was ransacked, my things, too. It was a real mess. Her apartment was hit, also. I'm sure you can find a police report on it. The perpetrators were never apprehended. The police thought whoever did it was looking for a list of volunteers. The irony, of course, is that Sheila would never have been organized enough to have a list."

"How about students, conflicts over grades, anything like that?"

"I know she's had some in the past. But I didn't witness anything in the last year or two."

"Monday's meeting, what time did you get to the meeting?" asked Elkins.

"About half past eight. I like to get there early so I can get a seat in the back."

"And you didn't see Professor Bensen on your way in?"

"No."

"When was the last time you saw her?"

"Late last week. I'd stopped in to Xerox some syllabi. We chatted briefly." She looked at Elkins, and anticipating his next question continued, "Just exchanged pleasantries, really. Neither one of us had taught this summer. Don't think I had seen her since June."

"And you didn't miss her at the meeting?"

"Quite frankly, I wasn't looking for her. It's a big department, over a hundred, counting adjuncts."

"Did you notice anyone leaving the lecture hall during the meeting?"

"No, but I'm not a good person to ask."

"How so?"

"I really hate meetings, and these are such a bore. Always take a book. Usually I don't notice much of anything."

"So you were sitting in the back. Were you one of the first people out?"

"No, I had stopped to talk to a friend. I was one of the last. When I got outside I could tell something dreadful had happened. Then David Jaymes said someone had jumped from the tower, and it looked like Sheila."

"And then?"

"I stood around with Seneca Carducci and a couple of other friends until the police arrived. Ms. Widdowson confirmed that it was Sheila. Then Chesterton arrived. He went right to Sheila. Knelt down next to her. Might have even touched her, I couldn't quite tell. Then I got out of there, went to the parking lot. I sat in my car for a long while, feeling faint. Eventually, I drove home and collapsed."

"We may have to reexamine Professor Bensen's papers in the course of the investigation. I hope we won't inconvenience you in the process."

"I'm sure it will be no problem." She waited a long moment and then asked, "Do you have other questions?"

"You have been very helpful. Anything else?" Char directed the question to Elkins.

"No. Thank you, Professor Castlemain for your assistance. If anything else occurs to you that might be useful to our inquiry, please call." He passed her a business card. "One more question, nothing to do with the investigation, just curiosity. What's your area of specialization?"

"My dissertation was a study of the foundations of Early English drama. But in recent years I've really focused on Restoration drama." She brightened as she responded to the question. Then she asked, "Do you want to go through Sheila's things now? Do you want me to leave?"

"We have other things that we need to do," Ray answered. "We will probably be back in a day or two."

"And you probably have a way of getting in," said Castlemain.

"Yes," Ray responded. "Is this a violation of your space? Is there some way...."

"No problem. Do what you need to do."

"Is there anything she didn't tell us?" Elkins asked as they stood just beyond the steps outside Old West.

"Lots. It was a wonderful performance. But then, it's not good to speak ill of the dead. Did you see that office? Bensen's side, what a mess. Those two women obviously had totally different styles."

"Okay. Okay. But is there anything she didn't tell us that might be important to this investigation?"

"Probably not. As she said, their only connection was that they shared space. One thing, who's Jean Brodie?"

"I'll buy you the video," said Ray, "after we get this mess cleaned up."

6

⌇⌇⌇⌇⌇

After Pascoe dropped Ray off at his car, he drove out to the gleaming new medical campus. He pulled into a lot marked "Medical Consultants Parking" near the rear of the complex. Although he had been to Dr. Gutiérrez's new office a few times, he consulted the map mounted on the wall inside the back entrance to confirm his memory. The pathology department was located on sublevel one at the rear of the medical center. As he walked through the long, clear hallways, he noticed that the place still smelled of new construction. The walls, flooring, ceiling materials, paints, and building mastics were still off-gassing a complex chemical bouquet, overpowering the usual hospital orders.

"Hope I didn't keep you waiting," Elkins entered the office of Dr. Kristin Gutiérrez, "Everything is taking more time than I thought it would."

"Isn't that always the way," she responded, as she pushed herself out of her swivel chair, hands on the arms, finally pulling herself to her full height.

Ray had first met her when he had requested help from the pathology department in teaching an advanced evidence course. At that time she was the newest and youngest pathologist on the Medical Center's staff and the only one with both an interest and a background in forensic pathology. In recent years Gutiérrez—tall, large-boned, a native Minnesotan of Swedish stock, married to Pablo Gutiérrez, a tiny Mexican, and the hospital's leading vascular surgeon—had lectured in Elkins's classes and, via the antiseptic medium of video, had demonstrated how a pathologist gathers evidence during an autopsy.

"And your timing's perfect. I'm running late also. Your office faxed over a copy of the incident report. I checked the temperature when the body was brought in. It's consistent with the time of the fall. I've done some preliminary work and had the body x-rayed. The films are in the autopsy room."

Elkins followed her the down the hall. Dressed in scrubs and running shoes, she exceeded Elkins's height. She opened the door and led him past the dissection table, covered with a sheet, to a long X-ray view box, the individual films already hanging against the backlit glass. She eyed his bare arms. "It's cool in here. Do you want a lab coat? It might help a little."

"No, I'm fine. Go ahead."

"It looks like she hit straight on. See how the skull is fractured, it's collapsing in." She used the blunt end of a Bic pen as a pointer. "There's also some damage here and in the first four vertebra, the next area to absorb the impact. We see this with motorcycle accidents. There's something else you'll find interesting," she said moving to the second and third films.

"What am I supposed to see?"

"Here, both sides, neither clavicle is fractured, same for the wrists and arms. Most people instinctively reach out, she didn't."

"And what do you make of that?"

"I don't know. It's just unusual."

"So she might have been dead before she hit she ground?"

"I didn't say that, Elkins," she responded, brushing a few stray hairs across her forehead and pushing them back under her surgical cap. She snapped on rubber gloves, the right hand first, then the left. Elkins stood at the side of the autopsy table.

"Continuing autopsy AUG-38," she said after pushing the red record switch. She pulled the sheet off the body. Elkins pulled back from the table.

"You okay?"

"Yes, go ahead," he said, looking at the waxy pallor of Bensen's naked body—the black hair on the deformed skull matted with dried blood, the narrow chest with boyish breasts, slender arms, hands with delicate fingers cased in plastic bags, a shallow belly rising to a thinly-haired pubis, frail legs, and delicate feet. Elkins was embarrassed. He thought it was voyeuristic to peek into the privacy that should be afforded the dead.

"The body," she looked at the notes on the clipboard, "has been identified as Sheila Bensen, a forty-year-old Caucasian female with black hair and hazel eyes. The body is 62 inches in length and weighs 102 pounds. Scar on upper left quadrant consistent with biopsy of breast tissue. Abrasion on left elbow with evidence of bleeding. Contusion on left heel.

Elkins kept his eyes on Gutiérrez, only occasionally glancing at the body. As a young homicide detective in Detroit, he had seen his share of autopsies. The dead were, for the most part, prostitutes, addicts, dealers, and gangbangers. People who put themselves in harm's way. People he didn't know, the likes of whom he had never known growing up in rural northern Michigan. It was only the occasional child that got to him, the innocents who caught a stray bullet during a drive-by shooting or a domestic. Thankfully, those had been few and far between. And he was young then, young enough to know he would never die.

"Massive damage to frontal and parietal bones." She checked the ears and nose. "Blood present in both ear canals and nose." She looked over at Elkins, studied him for a few seconds and then said, "I'm going to start with the head and then do the Y incision."

Ray nodded. The cold was starting to bother him. Then he felt almost feverish."I'll start with an inter-mastoid incision, but instead of going directly over the top, I'll make the incision this way so we can get a better view of the skull." She slipped the stainless blade through the flesh in front of the ear, circled the rear of the scalp, and continued back up around the ear. She ran the blade through a second time, making sure she had cut to the bone. Using both hands she peeled the scalp from the skull, covering the front of the face as she rolled the flesh forward.

A mild tremor ran through Elkins. Bensen's identity disappeared as her scalp was turned inside out.

"Multiple fractures of the skull, consistent with a fall from a great height." She looked at Elkins, observed his skin color for a few seconds, and pulling off a glove, reached over and turned off the recorder.

"Listen, before I open the skull, I can tell you what you want to know. Pending other discoveries, it looks like she died from the fall. Why don't you wait in my office until I finish this."

"That would be good," he said.

Firmly holding on to his elbow, Gutiérrez guided Elkins down the corridor to her office and got him settled in a chair. "Do you want something to drink? Coke, water?"

"Water, please."

She pulled a bottle of mineral water from a small refrigerator next to her desk and handed it to Elkins. "If you want to lie down, there's a cot in my dressing room." She opened a door on the right side of her office. He could see the cot. "There's a toilet in there also. It will take me another twenty or thirty minutes to finish up."

Elkins twisted the cap open and slowly sipped the water. When he felt less dizzy, he went into the next room and stretched out on the cot. He had always been impressed with how gentle Gutiérrez had been with some of his more squeamish students, never ridiculing or causing embarrassment. *I'll close my eyes for a few seconds,* he thought.

When he opened them again, he was covered with a blanket. He could hear the clicking of a keyboard in the next room. Gutiérrez looked up as he approached.

"How long was I out?"

"I don't know for sure, half an hour, maybe a bit more. You must have needed the sleep. When did you last observe an autopsy room?"

"Years, but...."

"Don't worry about it. I'm typing up my preliminary findings. Death was caused by a fall. The mechanism of death was massive destruction of brain tissue. The manner of death is still under investigation. I found no physical evidence of other injuries that might have preceded the fall. Her nails were clean, doesn't look like she was struggling with anyone. The full report should be transcribed by tomorrow afternoon."

"How about toxicology?"

"Week to ten days," she said pulling a blood pressure cuff from a drawer and wrapping it around his right arm.

"A tool of your trade?"

"Don't need it too often. Have to see if I can remember how these things work," she said with a chuckle as she inflated the cuff and held the round disk of the stethoscope against his arm. Elkins watched her eyes as she tracked the dial on the sphygmomanometer. She undid the cuff, wrapped it around his left arm, and repeated the procedure. Again, he followed her eyes. He saw what he took as a look of concern.

"What's the word?"

"As opposed to most of my patients, the good news is that you have a blood pressure," she offered with a soft smile. "How were you feeling when I walked you back to the office?"

"First I was cold, then hot, and I felt sort of dizzy."

"Have you had other episodes of dizziness recently?"

"There have been times I've felt a little light-headed, but nothing like this."

"Well, Elkins," she said as she sat on the corner of her desk. "Your blood pressure is way up. Has that ever been a problem before?"

"Never, it's always been normal or below. What does that have to do with...."

"Big fluctuations in blood pressure can cause dizziness, among other things. But of greater concern is that it increases your risk for heart attacks or strokes. When was the last time you saw your internist?"

"I don't know, maybe six or eight months ago," said Ray. "And your theory is that...."

"My tentative diagnosis is that you were hypertensive when you arrived, and viewing the autopsy, for some reason, exacerbated the condition. Who is your internist?"

"Ron Glass."

"Tell me again, when did you last see him?"

"Maybe a year, maybe longer."

"You know, Ray, this is getting to be a pretty big city, especially compared to ten years ago when I first arrived. But it's also a highly stratified place. People like us—you, me, my husband, Ellen—end up being connected. We're in overlapping groups. The sociologists probably have some name for it. As you know, my husband is a big devotee of chamber music. He was a big fan of her quartet. As you remember, we saw you at all her local concerts over the years. What I'm trying to say is that I know about her illness, and I have a sense of what you went through while she was dying. There's an emotional toll and a physical toll. You're probably still dealing with both of them. And you're entering middle age. Our bodies start to change, and usually not for the better. You should see Ron Glass. Promise me you'll do that, Ray."

"I'll make an appointment," he responded without enthusiasm, climbing out of his chair. "Just as soon as I get this case under control."

"Do what I tell you," she said with a mocking earnestness, "or you'll end up in there," she pointed toward the autopsy room, "sooner than you should."

7

Ray had stopped for a sandwich and a soda before leaving the medical center. By the time he reached Bensen's apartment to meet Pascoe, he was feeling much better. She was standing beside her car in the parking lot near Bensen's apartment waiting for him. They stood and chatted, neither one inclined to rush into the task at hand.

"I'm glad you're here. I went up to the apartment with the manager," said Pascoe. "He was checking to make sure he had the right key, but I didn't want to go in until you got here. This gives me the creeps."

"Why's that?" asked Elkins.

"Going into Bensen's space, looking through her things. This is one part of police work I've never been comfortable with, going through the detritus of other people's lives."

"It's not invasive like an autopsy," said Ray. A vision of Bensen's naked body on the dissection table flashed in front of him, a wave of revulsion moved through his flesh. He pushed the specter back and focused on their immediate task. "We're just looking through her things for possible clues." He paused briefly, "Think of it as a garage sale."

"I hate garage sales."

"So do I," he admitted looking carefully at Pascoe. She wasn't as young as he had remembered. There was a sadness creeping at the edges of her deep brown eyes, an ancient look of suffering in the early stages.

Pascoe returned his gaze. "We're a lot alike. That's probably why you hired me," she said with a soft quiet laugh. "Besides a suicide note, what are you looking for?

"I'm not quite sure yet," he said. "I need to get a better sense of Bensen. Maybe something will leap out at us. Also, check for prints."

"In case of what?"

"Her death turns out to be something other than suicide. I'm looking for matching prints here and at the carillon that aren't Bensen's."

"You're interesting to watch," she said. "From the beginning you've never assumed it was a suicide. I think it is. What am I missing?"

"Missing," he mused, "nothing. It's just a feeling."

"Feeling. I thought we were supposed to be hard-nosed collectors of empirical data, professionals led by data, not feelings."

"Did you know I was an English major into my junior year?" asked Elkins.

"Your ADD is kicking in. Let's stay on the topic," said Pascoe

"The empirical side is extremely important, but only part of the picture. Our work often demands that we put ourselves into the head of the person we're investigating. We have to put ourselves into their story. What are they feeling, what's their history, and what do they care about? In this case the facts say suicide. Be suspicious of the obvious." He paused briefly, "Well, that was didactic as hell."

"Almost patronizing, but since you're the boss, I'll humor you," Pascoe said shrugging her shoulders. "So let's play your game. If I were going to kill myself, what outward manifestations might someone find in my apartment? Conversely, if I weren't going to off myself, how might that be reflected? I don't know if this game will turn up anything, but at least it makes the task less odious."

They entered the building and climbed the stairs to Bensen's second story apartment. Elkins turned the key in the lock and pushed the door open. The blinds were closed. The room was hot, the air stagnant. Three walls of the living room were covered with bookcases, boards and bricks, each crammed with books, magazines, and journals—some standing on end, others stacked sideways. A glut of books and magazines covered an overstuffed, vinyl-covered chair and the couch, a low-end vestige of the Danish modern school.

"Guess she didn't entertain much," Pascoe caught his eye.

"Standing room only."

A small chrome-legged Formica table was covered with mail, much of it looking unopened. Elkins pushed it around with the back of a pencil.

"You'll want me to go through this."

"Yes, looks like mostly bills, but you never know."

Elkins inspected the stove and opened the refrigerator, catching the lip of the door with the pencil. It was empty save three bottles of mineral water, two full, one empty: a half-head of lettuce; and a pint carton of skimmed milk. "Must have just gotten the milk. Expiration date is Saturday." He pushed open the freezer. Seven frozen dinners, all fried chicken, and three chicken pot-pies.

"Wasn't much of a housekeeper," said Pascoe.

"Or cook, and no gourmet," he responded.

"How could you not be depressed by this place? No color, no art, place is a mess, and frozen dinners."

They moved to the bedroom, small and cluttered with piles of clothes. A bike leaned against one wall—black, three speed, with a weathered wicker basket attached to the handle bars. Panties and bras were draped over the bike.

"A drying rack?" he asked.

"A rather novel approach, sort of a nice decorating touch. Might just catch on."

"Does this look the place of someone planning on killing herself?" he asked.

"How would you know?"

He pointed at the bed. "She didn't make it."

"Did you make yours?"

"I pulled the blankets up. I usually do that."

"Blacks and grays, inexpensive labels," said Pascoe as she looked at the hanging clothes. "Everything is worn. Didn't seem to care about clothes. Probably wasn't working with very much money. What does an assistant professor make?"

"They start in the low forties and don't get much of an increase until they get promoted to associate."

"So you spend how many years?" Char asked.

"Seven."

"Seven years at an entry level salary. I've got much to learn. As a student you're just not aware of life on the other side of the desk."

"Aspirin, Tylenol, two half-used prescriptions for antibiotics, Band-Aids, tooth paste, brush, comb, deodorant, " Elkins listed the contents of the medicine chest as he stood in the small bathroom. Pascoe slid behind him. He felt her breasts touch his back as she peered over his shoulder. He moved forward slightly.

"No make-up, nail polish, perfume, nothing feminine." She turned and looked over the shelves. "Extra toilet paper, shampoo, conditioner, and an unopened box of Tampax.

"So explain this to me, you get a Ph.D. and get an entry level salary for seven years. Then what?" asked Pascoe as they made a final survey of the living room.

"You might get tenured if…"

"If what?" asked Pascoe.

"If you've done the right things professionally, if you haven't screwed up politically, and if your department has the funding for a tenure position."

"And what happens if you don't. What was Sheila's future?"

"Don't know enough about Sheila to tell you. But, generally speaking, you might get lucky and find another tenure track position, usually at a smaller school. And the money would be less."

"And if you're not lucky?"

"People get one-year gigs covering for someone on sabbatical. Others do adjunct work. The pay is lousy, so they teach lots of sections at three or four different schools, live in their cars. A few get jobs at community colleges. And some, probably the smart ones, get out of academe and do something else. That's probably better than being a gypsy professor for the rest of their working lives."

"So this is life in the ivy tower. Given what she had to look forward to, I can see why she jumped." She gave Elkins a wry smile.

Ray sat in his car for several minutes after Pascoe drove away, making notes in a steno pad. In the process of putting the ballpoint back into his shirt pocket, he noticed a folded piece of paper. He pulled it out and opened the grocery list that he had been adding onto for days. He remembered that before leaving for the office he had put it in his pocket thinking that he would stop for groceries on the way home. So much had happened since then, and he was in no mood to spend a half an hour or more in a crowded store. He would make do with whatever was in the house.

Later, standing in front of a near empty refrigerator, he thought perhaps he should've gone shopping. Other than condiments, some dead lettuce, and a near empty jar of thimbleberry jam, there was little to eat. He found a package of frozen enchiladas in the freezer and tossed them in the microwave. As they circled the interior, he pulled the *New York Times* from its blue plastic bag and scanned the front page. Eventually he carried the steaming enchiladas, now on the dinner plate, and a beer out to the deck. Picking at the food, he continued working his way through the paper.

Dinnertime had once been a major part of his life with Ellen. It was the period when they would catch up with one another. Ray did most of the cooking, something he enjoyed, while Ellen made the salad and handled the cleanup. Since her death he had almost stopped cooking.

By the time he had read through most of the national news, his dinner had gone cold. Next he turned to the international news, his concentration interrupted by the sudden appearance of Clifford Chesterton, slightly out of breath, carrying a bright yellow plastic cooler.

"May I join you?" he asked climbing onto the deck.

"Please do," Ray responded.

"I know it's rather late," he eyed the mostly uneaten enchiladas, "but Stephanie was wondering if you'd like to join us for dinner. She's made a crown roast of lamb, and says you're a great fan of that."

"I won't turn you down," said Ray. "She knows my vulnerabilities when it comes to food."

"Well, she told me you'd say 'yes.' And she's running a bit late, so I thought we'd have a drink or two while we're waiting for her to finish up." Chesterton opened the cooler and pulled out a bottle of scotch, and one of soda, two Whiskey glasses, and a Ziploc bag filled with crescent shaped ice cubes. He added ice to both glasses, added three fingers of the amber liquor, splashed some soda in his glass, and passed the second tumbler and the soda bottle to Ray.

"I'm a couple drinks ahead of you," said Chesterton. "Today was a hard day. I'm trying to figure it all out."

"Any conclusions?" asked Ray.

"No, more questions than answers. I'm tired of thinking about it. I need to talk about something else and let it rest a while." He pushed his feet out and slid down his chair. He surveyed the scene in silence for a long moment, then sipped his drink and looked over at Ray. "It's very pleasant up here, isn't it, the nicest place in town. The only bit of terrain in the whole region." They sat in silence for a while, then Chesterton said, "You know, we've been neighbors for a good while. Our women were the best of friends. I think their schedules were more open. They spent time together during the day when we were off doing other things. We've never really gotten to know one another. I was thinking about that after our talk at the hospital, that we have never talked much other than the mostly empty chatter at social gatherings." He finished his drink and set the tumbler on the table. "Ready for another?"

"I haven't finished this one," said Ray.

"Let me top it up for you," responded Chesterton as he mixed a drink for himself. "How did you end up here, out on this vast prairie?"

"Like most people," answered Ray. "I completed my graduate degree, and there was a job here. I initially thought I would move on after a few years."

"Didn't we all," laughed Chesterton. "What were you doing before that?"

"The short history. I was in graduate school, before that I was a cop in Detroit for a few years. It was interesting work, but I couldn't imagine spending my life there. And before that the army. I was in the military police, mostly in Europe. How about you?"

"Not quite ditto, the particulars differ, but a variation on the same story. I was finishing graduate school in Chicago. I had been sort of a wunderkind, three articles in the *Shakespeare Quarterly* before I even finished my dissertation. I thought I was on my way to a major school. My dissertation became a well-reviewed book. I was here by then. But I thought some large school would pick me up. Even then, the market in English was lousy, but I was sure I would get recruited to a pretty good place."

"But how did you end up here in the first place," asked Ray.

"Well, my dissertation advisor was a friend of Keith Beckner, who chaired this department back then. Keith was extremely entrepreneurial. He really knew how to work foundations: Ford, Carnegie, Rockefeller. I think I mentioned this earlier today when we were at the hospital. Beckner had this dream about making this university the preeminent center for the study of English literature in America. Don't ask me where that came from. But he had sold his dream to the grant officers from several major foundations and the university administration. The department was awash in cash. So my chair, looking around at the bleak job market for new PhDs, counseled me to come here. He thought it was an up-and-coming department, and that I could use it as a stepping-stone to my next job. And once I got here, Beckner mentored me like crazy. I got tenure and promotion quickly and became the associate chair within a few years. When he moved on to Provost, he paved the way for me to follow him as chair.

"How about the Center for the Study of…."

"It didn't succeed. We built it, and they didn't come. We were never able to attract the large number of graduate students that he anticipated. The money and the enthusiasm quickly went away." Chesterton tossed the ice cubes from his now empty glass onto the lawn and retrieved several fresh ones from the cooler. He poured more whiskey into the glass and added a bit of soda, stirring the mixture with his index finger. He looked over at Ray. "Are you ready for another?"

"I shouldn't. I'm already feeling smashed."

"Then you should have another," said Chesterton. He refilled Ray's glass and pushed it across the glass-topped table. "Were you with Ellen when you came here?"

"No, but I met her soon after, and we quickly became a couple."

"It's none of my damn business, and you can tell me to go to hell, but why didn't you two ever marry?"

"She was married when we met, not living with a him, but still married. He was some sort of crazy, a physicist. He had been fighting the divorce for several years. In fact, we did not move in together until the divorce was final. And I wanted to marry her. I asked her many times. Her answer was always the same. 'Why should we ruin a good thing?' Near the end I proposed again, and she said she had always been happy with the way things were. She said the important thing was how we treated one another, not whether we had a contract to be together." Ray swirled the drink in his glass. "How about you and Stephanie? She's not your first wife?"

Chesterton looked at Ray and laughed. "You know, we wouldn't be having this conversation if we weren't both a little bit tight. Ah yes, I was married to someone before, nice woman, someone from graduate school. The first few years here she wrote her dissertation. She was very qualified, but she couldn't get a job in my department because there was an anti-nepotism policy at the university at that time. She went into the job market and got a job at Johns Hopkins. We had an airplane marriage for a number of years, much longer than we should have. She eventually found someone else. And I had a few romances before Stephanie. She was a graduate student. We've had good years together. My cancer a few years back changed things...."

"But there is medicine for that...."

"Too much damage, too much damage from both the surgery and radiation therapy. They gave me my life back, but there was a price. Stephanie is a vital young woman. So we talked about it." Chesterton finished his drink and set it back on the table. "To outsiders it might look sort of peculiar."

Ray said nothing. He just sat there holding onto his glass, gazing into his yard and beyond.

"Are you two men ready for dinner yet?" asked Stephanie as she emerged from the twilight.

"Well, we've settled most of the major problems in the world," Chesterton responded. "But if we don't get some food soon, I think we may pass out."

8

Wednesday morning arrived too early. Elkins was always awake by six, so he was startled when he looked at his watch and saw that it was almost 8:00 A.M. He laid in bed for several more minutes, placing the cool palm of his right hand on his throbbing forehead.

He stood in the shower longer than usual, and forced himself to eat a granola bar with his coffee before leaving the house.

Elkins settled into a waiting room chair in the Professional Arts Building adjacent to the Medical Center a few minutes before 9:00. He rummaged through the pile of magazines on the end table next to his seat . His choices were limited to dog-eared copies of *Time, Car and Driver, Sports Illustrated, Sailing,* and *Better Homes and Gardens*—all three or more months out of date.

He had just started reading an article on who would win the NBA championship—a championship that had been decided several months before—when the door to the inner office opened and Dr. Margrave came out to greet him. Elkins had met Margrave when Ellen was in the final stages of breast cancer. The doctor led the death and dying group at the medical center. After Ellen's death, Elkins had also been in individual therapy with him for months.Margrave ushered him into his consultation room. There were two chairs in the room, one facing a window that looked out over the back of the medical center, the other off to the side facing the first. As Elkins settled into the chair facing the window he said, "Since I'll be asking the questions this time, perhaps we should change chairs."

"This one was built for me," said Margrave with a smile. "It's bigger."

Before he met Margrave, Elkins had a stereotypical view of what a psychiatrist should look like: a male, small in frame, with delicate features, burning eyes, and perhaps a goatee. Margrave didn't fit that stereotype; he was a big man, tall, broad shouldered, with red hair and freckles. Although in his late forties, his physique had changed little from his college basketball days.

What had impressed Elkins in both group and individual therapy was Margrave's ability to ask questions that focused the discussion. Ray felt that it would have taken him months longer to work through his grief without Margrave's help.

Margrave pointed to a thick manila folder on the table next to his chair. "After you called, I reviewed Bensen's file."

"How long was she a patient of yours?"

"She started with me about five years ago." He paused and rummaged through the folder for a few moments, " Yes, it was late September, five years ago."

"It appears that we're dealing with a suicide. Anything that you can tell me about her that doesn't violate your professional ethics relative to...."

"I can answer questions relative to dates and times, I can't discuss anything relative to what was said during our sessions. I'm checking with our ethicist and attorney as to what I can tell you."

"I appreciate that fact. When did she enter therapy?"

"As I said, I started seeing her about five years ago. It was in late September. At that time her mother was dying. I can't tell you much more than that."

"How long was she in therapy with you?"

"Almost constantly. And that goes against one of my major beliefs. I don't want patients to be dependent on me. Sheila was, and I wasn't very successful at extricating myself." Margrave stopped and looked at Elkins. "I'm fairly eclectic in my approach. I try to get people functioning quickly. Even though my training was Freudian, I don't find that approach useful for most of my patients; I'll use it occasionally if I'm convinced it's the only thing that's going to work. I ended up involving Sheila in analysis because I thought that if I could get her through her childhood, I might eventually get her to shed that baggage so we could focus on her current problems."

Elkins broke a long silence, "And?"

"And that didn't quite work. It wasn't especially effective. That baggage was too important to her. She wouldn't let go. She needed a fix of it every day to rationalize the way she dealt with the world."

"Did you see her recently?"

"I was gone most of July and early August, so we didn't have our usual appointments. I did see her for forty-five minutes last week and the week before."

"Was she suicidal?"

"This is one of those odd things. If I were in her situation, I would be suicidal, but I don't think that she was."

"I'm not following," said Elkins.

"Here's a woman in her forties. She's in her last year here, her second last year if you know what I mean. They gave her an additional year because her tenure appeals dragged into the next calendar year. She's burned all her bridges professionally. She would have had a difficult time ever getting another job in her field, a field where there aren't a lot of jobs to begin with." He lifted both hands in the air and gestured with agitation, "Yet, she wasn't upset. I was. She denied the reality of her situation. I was concerned because she wasn't dealing with it and wasn't making plans about what she was going to do next. She was denying that there was any problem."

"Could she have suddenly come to that realization and decided the only way out was suicide?" asked Elkins.

"I've speculated on that. I mean, who's to say for sure. But in the years that I've known her, she never let reality intervene very much. So the question I have to ask is, why now? Of course, these things are not unheard of. People deny their reality for years and then suddenly take some action. But a suicide doesn't seem right. Killing yourself in front of your colleagues, all theatre. Showing them what they've driven you to. Sheila was a master at inflicting guilt, but with language, not action." He stopped and looked at Ray. "Have you found a suicide note?"

"No, not yet."

"If she were going to kill herself, I would have expected a carefully crafted letter where she identified all those she thought had hurt her, a letter in which she elaborated on every incident where she felt she had been snubbed or harmed. But I have to give you this caveat. I've learned in this business to expect the unexpected. However, her suicide just doesn't feel right." He gave Ray a long look, "Changing the subject, how are you doing?"

"I'm okay."

"How okay?"

"Most of the time, during the day I'm fine. It's just late at night and early in the morning when I get blue, especially in the morning. There are still lots of ghosts."

Are you still taking the prescription...?"

"No, I stopped a couple of months ago. I don't think I need pills."

"Elkins, grieving takes time. Two or three years, sometimes more. Have you given any additional thought to moving to another house, a new environment? You might be able to leave some of the ghosts behind."

"I'm comfortable there. It's a beautiful house. Besides the thought of moving—I hate packing." Ray was feeling uncomfortable.

"Have the place torched." Margrave chuckled. "You can take the insurance money and buy new. No packing, no unpacking. You once talked about moving back to the area where you spent your childhood, northern Michigan as I remember it."

"Yes, good memory. That's a fantasy. I really love it there, but there are no jobs for someone with my credentials. Maybe when I retire."

"You need some distance. What's important to you? What will make you happy?"

"Let me go back to Benson," said Ray. "From your professional view, a suicide is unlikely."

"You're forcing me to equivocate a bit, but it's a prerogative of the professional. We're almost as bad as lawyers. If she killed herself, I'm surprised. That said, this is a very imperfect science. You never know what someone might do."

9

~~~~~

The heat of a late summer day was beginning to build as Elkins drove the freshly paved six-lane ribbon of concrete back into town toward central campus. He passed the several miles of new subs that had sprung up in recent years, circling the city like annual rings in a tree trunk. The fields of corn and soybeans had been pushed back, replaced with vinyl-clad two story homes on treeless lots. At the border of the original city limits, the highway abutted against the warren of roads and alleys that had been laid out more than a hundred years before. The once wide thoroughfares of the horse and buggy era were now the congested arteries of the densely populated town.

Ray parked in a near-empty faculty lot and stopped by a Starbucks for a large coffee and raspberry scone. The coffee and food seemed to help lessen the effects of the hangover. He started to go to his car, and then decided he could use the walk. The campus religious center was in an area of newer buildings on the east side of the central campus. Most of the buildings in the area had been erected in the 60s on land reclaimed from old homes and apartments, when enrollments exploded with the arrival of the baby boomers. Most of the steel framed, concrete block buildings were faced with thin tan bricks, aluminum, and glass, built in a style that started looking dated and dowdy a decade or two later.

The center was built in the style of its neighbors, streamlined gothic windows and doors suggested the edifice's devotional intent. Ray stood for a moment in the cool, dull interior, waiting for his eyes to adjust. Then he followed the signs to the office of Father Robert Durning—known on campus as Father Bob—at the back of the building on the lower level. The door to the office was ajar, and Ray could hear Father Bob. "Listen, I've got an appointment in a few minutes. I'll get back to you tomorrow with an answer, okay? God bless."

Ray knocked and pushed the door open. Father Bob stood up and reached across the desk to shake hands. "Please," he motioned to one of the two unoccupied chairs, "have a seat."

Elkins settled into the chair, the same chair he had sat in when he and Father Bob had discussed the details of Ellen's funeral. He was struck again by the intense blue of Father Bob's eyes, the color heightened by his deep tan and his thick blond hair.

"You mentioned on the phone that you wanted to talk about Sheila Benson. Don't know how much I can tell you. It's strange, really. I had almost daily contact with the woman, but I can't say I ever really learned much about her."

"Well, just start by telling me about the daily contact," said Ray.

"As you know, this is an ecumenical campus ministry. My office is here, but I conduct services at our campus chapel down the street. We don't have an organized altar guild like a regular parish. Sheila filled that role. She came in every morning about six-thirty and helped me with the seven o'clock mass. This has been going on for years, long before I arrived. She hardly ever missed a day."

"How long have you been here?"

"This is the start of my fourth year."

"So, she was here on Monday morning?"

"Yes," Father Bob answered. Elkins waited until it became clear Father Bob wasn't going to say anything more.

"Monday, did you notice anything unusual?"

"No, she was here when I arrived and had taken care of everything. I'm not much of a morning person. I come in, do the Mass. It's a ritual, it's sort of automatic, and then I go down to the Brown Jug. After an hour of coffee, breakfast, and the paper, then I'm fully awake."

"How did she get in?"

"She had her own key." Father Bob slid back in his chair, pulling his athletic frame into a more erect posture.

"To the exterior door?"

"Well, actually I've never thought about it. She must have had keys for most of the doors. She would need several."

"How many?"

"Let's see. One for the chapel door, it's kept locked during the night. Another for the vestry. And then she had a key for the storage cabinet where we keep the wine, communion wafers, chalices, and other valuables. Again, before I arrived, there were several instances of theft and vandalism, so we have this heavy steel cabinet to keep things safe. So that's three keys.

"You gave her...."

"No, I didn't give her anything. Sheila came with the Ministry. She had performed the same function for Father Timothy. He probably gave her the keys. If you need to know, I could find out where he is, and you could pursue it with him."

"Monday, did you see her leave?"

"I don't remember. Days blend. As I said, after the service I go down to the Jug."

"How many people were at the service?"

"There are never many, as few as three or four, occasionally around ten. And I'm not sure about Monday. They're mostly foreign students—usually from South America, Asia, and Africa—occasionally a staff or faculty member. Our kids don't like to get up that early. But then, I didn't either when I was a college boy," he gave Elkins a wry smile.

"Can you remember anyone who was here Monday morning? Someone I might talk to. Are there any regulars?

"Monday morning was a bit of a disaster, and the subsequent events have made things even more of a blur." He opened his hands.

"How so," Elkins pushed, hearing impatience creeping into his voice as he moved forward in his chair."I was out with a friend till very late. I'm afraid I had a very bad hangover," he said sheepishly. "It's been years since I've had a head like that." He ran his right hand along his temple, pushing his carefully styled hair back. Elkins noted the early hints of a receding hairline.

"Let me return to Professor Bensen," pressed Ray, locking his eyes on Father Bob's. "Is there anything else you can tell me about her?"

"What do you want to know?"

"Your relationship with her, how did you get along?"

"If truth be told, when it came to Sheila, I was of two minds. Here in the church she was wonderful. She was pleasant, helpful, and almost too willing to please. But when I would meet her in other settings she was a completely different person. Sheila was schizoid." He stopped again and waited, letting the word hang.

"How so?"

"Let me give you an example," his elbows now resting on the desk, he brought his hands together, interlacing his fingers in a prayer-like pose. "Earlier this year I was part of a panel discussing the role of women in the clergy—it was one of those colloquies put on by the Inter-faith Council—and Sheila, representing a women's group, was also on the panel. It was dreadful. I don't think that I, personally, have ever been so bitterly attacked." He stopped and waited again for Elkins to pursue. Elkins was feeling annoyed by the game.

"Yes?"

"Her attack was really against the Catholic Church, but it was directed at me, and she expected me to answer for the Church." Father Bob's face reddened, and his voice rose in pitch. "Sheila was vicious, holding me accountable for two thousand years of history. It was all about the oppression of women by the Church, a church controlled by, to paraphrase her, a bunch of old white men committed to the subservience of women. And that was just her opening gambit. She got into the Church's position on birth control as another weapon of oppression. The most difficult thing wasn't her arguments, it was her anger. I've never confronted that kind of hostility. Talk about cognitive dissonance. Here," he opened his hands, fingers forward, palms up, "she was the overly deferential helper, but on the outside she referred to us as a bunch of oppressive bastards."

"Did you think she was capable of a violent act?"

"No. Well, I shouldn't say that. After that confrontation it crossed my mind. In a society with so many guns floating around, there's always that possibility." He brought his hands together again.

"Do you know anything about her private life, who her friends were, was she in any relationships?"

"No, not really. All I know about her is hearsay," Father Bob responded, his tone calming. "I don't think she liked men, or at least had relationships with men. And I don't know about her relationships with women."

"Are you suggesting...?"

"I'm not suggesting anything. I know so little of Sheila beyond our relationship here. Anything I might say about her sexual orientation would only be conjecture on my part." He gently rapped the knuckles of his right hand on the desk.

"Given your training and experience in counseling, would you speculate on why Professor Bensen might have taken her own life?"

As I've told you several times," he offered in an irritated tone. "I didn't really know her. Her death is a tragedy. If I thought that she was suicidal, I would have made every effort to reach out to her. In the past I've attempted to build a relationship with her, but she was inaccessible. Now I feel guilty that I didn't do more, didn't try harder, but I don't think I could have ever reached her. Her problems were deeper than I had suspected."

"Let me go over some old ground again. You don't remember seeing her leave on Monday?"

"Everything sort of blends together." He paused, looking at his fingertips as he bounced them together, his wrists now resting on the edge of the desk. "I think I was talking to a couple of worshipers after the Mass. I don't remember seeing her go. This was the nature of our relationship. She came in and performed her duties, but we didn't talk very often. That's the way she wanted it."

"What time would she have left?"

"7:25, 7:30 at the latest. It's a very short service."

Elkins slid one of his cards across the desk, "You know where to reach me. If you have any more thoughts about Monday, or anything else that you think might be useful, please give me a call." He started to rise.

"Before you go. There's something I don't understand," said Father Bob, his eyes on Elkins's in a hard stare.

"What don't you...?"

"Why are you going to all this trouble when the woman obviously killed herself?"

"This is an unexplained death," answered Ray. "We investigate all such deaths to eliminate the possibility of foul play."

"Is there any suggestion...?"

"No, not at this time," said Ray, pushing himself out of his chair. He stopped at the door and held Father Bob in his gaze for a long moment, "Thank you for your help."

Father Bob nodded, but said nothing more, turning his attention to a stack of papers on his desk.

Ray was glad to get out into the sun. Father Bob made him uncomfortable. Perhaps it was the memory of Ellen's funeral. Father Bob had gone on and on about how glad Ellen was to be with Jesus. Ray wasn't sure. Ellen was a fallen-away Catholic who, even at the end, showed no interest in renewing her faith. In her final weeks Father Bob visited her at the hospice. Ray had the impression that she found Bob annoying. She said he was, "too pretty" to be a priest. However, at the end Ellen had asked for a Catholic funeral. She said her mother would find comfort in that.

10

Ray was happy to get back into the sunshine and warmth of the day, away from the dull light and chill of the air-conditioned building. He retrieved his car and drove over to University Maintenance, a complex that occupied a two-block area on the north side of campus that housed the power plant, repair and trade shops, storage facilities, and a management building.

Ray found John Stockton, the Director of University Maintenance, in his littered office near the main entrance of the one-story cement-block building.

"I was expecting you a bit earlier," said Stockton, as he stood and extended his hand.

"Just running a bit behind," Ray replied, dropping into a chair. "When I sent you that e-mail yesterday...."

"Isn't that always the way. Every afternoon before I leave work I write a to-do list for the next day. Then I get here, and all I do is fight fires, one little crisis after another. At the end of the day I look at the list, and I haven't accomplished any of those things. Frustrating as hell. So you want to know about the lock and key system."

"I want to know how Sheila Benson, the woman who jumped from the carillon, got a key for the building."

"How she got a key, that's an interesting question. The person who can best explain our rather cobbled together system is Ben Beyer. He's been in charge of keys since the 60s, think he was right out of high school then. In the beginning, he was a university carpenter and looking after keys was just sort of an extra assignment. I think he's been doing it full-time more than thirty years. Could have retired ten years ago, but he's stayed on, and I'm damn glad. He knows everything about the locks and keying systems at this place, and none of it is documented. I've tried to get him to start writing things down, but he says he's always too busy, and I think that's probably true. When he does finally retire, we'll be in an even bigger mess." Stockton stood. Come on, I'll take you over there."

Ben Beyer had his back to them when they entered the lock shop. He was cutting a key and didn't notice them until he switched off the machine and turned to get something off his desk.

"Didn't see you boys there," he said.

"Just arrived and didn't want to interrupt you. Ben, this here's Elkins from University Police. He's investigating that death over at the carillon, and he's got some questions about keys."

"Horrible thing," said Beyers. "I've been around here a long time, and I can never remember anything like that. Was she some kind of wacko or something?"

"We're trying to figure it out," said Ray. "I need to know about the key system." He held out the key in the plastic bag. "That's an AC001 key," Ben looked at the key through the bag.

"What does that mean?" asked Elkins.

"A bit of history here. It's one of the old series. There wasn't any key system until the 50s when the college started to grow real fast. That's when they put in the first key system. It was used in all the new buildings, and they eventually converted most of the locks in the old buildings. It's a real simple system, or at least it was in the beginning. The master key that would open everything had the AC001, 'AC' for 'All Campus' and the '001' was, well, I'm not sure. The other keys had letters and numbers to identify buildings and rooms. Faculty members get a key to their office and that key also opens the exterior door of the building. Department chairs have a key that opens all the doors in their department, deans have the same kind of thing, but for the area they manage.

"When we became a university in the early 60s that master code was changed to 'AU'. So I can tell you that key," he pointed to the key in the plastic bag, "is from before sixty-two. There are very few of those around anymore. The 'AUs' will open the 'ACs', but it won't work the other way."

"Who has access to master keys?"

"Pretty much limited to maintenance people: custodians, electricians, plumbers, the supervisors in the paint and carpentry shops. Police and fire have them, too."

"How many of the master keys are in circulation?" asked Elkins.

"Can't tell you for sure. We've ordered thousands of blanks, maybe tens of thousands over the years. I've never kept records of how many of a given key I cut, but I've made a lot of those. You know, we have people that need them day to day, and keys get lost. People quit and take them along. Contractors, they're the worst, they don't return them. Given how many are probably floating out there, I guess we're damn lucky we don't have more problems."

"How about the carillonneur?"

"That's ole Percival Pennington, but he don't have a master. He's got a key for just that building. He has a second key for his office and the entrance doors in the music school. He loses his keys at least once a year, usually more, and the replacements I give him are just cut for those doors. Let me show you." He went to one of several gray metal cabinets hanging on the wall, opened it, turned several hinged leaves, like pages in a book, and removed two keys held together on a thin metal ring. "I always do both his keys, his office and the carillon, as a set. And I make up several sets at a time, knowing he'll be needing them." Beyer lifted a key set off the hook. He removed one of the keys from the ring. He turned several leaves in the storage cabinet and removed a second key. He put this key against the key that would only open the carillon door. "Look at these two. If you compare that AC001 with this one, you can see the difference."

"Yes, I see it. So Pennington would never have had an AC001?"

Beyer rubbed his chin as he thought about the question. "Well, if truth be told, I might have given him an AC001 a time or two over the years. I always have an inventory of those. And in that particular lock in the carillon, they work better. That lock never gets enough use. It's always cranky. The master key works better. Besides, I wasn't worried about Professor Pennington running around campus opening doors he shouldn't."

Beyer picked up the plastic bag holding the key Ray had brought in and inspected it closely again. "I guess the mystery you gotta solve is how that woman got the AC001. And, like I said, over the years a lot of those went out of here. And given the looks of that one, it's seen a lot of miles."

~~~~~~

11

Thursday morning Elkins sipped on a mug of coffee as Char Pascoe briefed him on a long list of items. Working toward her summary, she leafed through pages of a legal pad to check her notes.

"Pennington is still at his place in northern Minnesota. This is according to the dean's secretary in the music school. He had a heart attack in early August. They hope he will be back and well enough to play in the next couple of weeks. She told me that he has been emeritus for almost ten years, but he continues on as the carillonneur. She said he usually comes back to campus the week before the first home football game. I guess that won't be true this year."

"They don't have anyone else?"

"I asked that question."

"And?"

"It was just weird, like Pennington has always been here. No one expected that he wouldn't show up. She said they were scrambling for a possible replacement." Char paused briefly, "I did get his number, and I called him in Minnesota. I wanted to know if anyone else had a key to the carillon."

"And?"

"Pennington said that in recent years he's the only one that's ever in the carillon other than the maintenance people. The public tours stopped years ago, something about the stairs and lighting, a question of safety and liability. He said that he used to give graduate students keys so they could practice, but he said these days few students want to learn how to play a carillon. Then he told me when he's dead, they'll just put some long haired kid up there with an electric guitar and big speakers."

"Did you tell him what happened?"

"I had to. He wanted to know why the police were so interested in who had keys. I told him and could tell the news upset him."

"Well that's understandable. What a violation of his space." Ray paused for a long moment, then asked, "What else?"

"I've got prints for Bensen, and they matched the ones on the key and the chair. I've also had a phone conversation with Dr. Gutiérrez."

"And," said Elkins.

"She wanted you to know about an interesting finding."

"Okay?"

"Gutiérrez said she found partially dissolved calcium tablets in Bensen's stomach."

"What?"

"Calcium tablets, you know, women, osteoporosis. It looks like Bensen had her vitamins and minerals with her breakfast. So why would you bother if you were going to kill yourself?"

"Who knows? We're all such creatures of habit." Elkins paused and sipped his coffee. "Or she hadn't planned to kill herself."

"So what are you thinking, a capricious act? She decided to kill herself on a whim sometime after breakfast?"

"If this was suicide, it wasn't capricious. She had somehow acquired a key, thought about how she was going to do it. That wouldn't have been her first trip in. But what if this was a murder?"

"We don't have any evidence." She looked and asked with emphasis, "Do we?"

"Well, no, but we always have to keep that possibility out there."

"For a reasonable time," said Char. "But if there's no evidence to the contrary, you've got to reach some kind of... Looking at your face I can tell you're not comfortable."

"I just have this feeling, and I don't have data to support it. Until we do, we keep saying it's an apparent suicide. Anything else?"

Pascoe flipped through the papers again, reading as she went. She looked up and said, "It seems to me there was one more thing, but I can't remember it. Oh yes, Bensen's car. It was parked in the main campus faculty parking ramp."

Elkins nodded to signal that he took in the information.

"You have someone waiting to see you," said Pascoe. "I told her I'd make sure she was next."

"Who?"

"Reda Rudd. Says she's from the *Daily*."

"Reda, haven't seen her during the summer months. She's the one who wrote the exposé of the athletic department and the university police. And," he added, "she created an opportunity to bring one of the criminal justice program's top graduates back to campus. Wave her in on your way out."

"Sure will. And," she gave Elkins a mocking smile, "I'll thank her for giving you the opportunity to persuade me to take a major pay cut for the honor of returning to my alma mater."

"Cost of living is less here. You'll be ahead in the long run. Plus, when you start your Ph.D., you'll get a tuition waver."

"I can hardly wait," she retorted. "I just don't have enough to do."

"Reda, come on in. Want some coffee?"

Reda—wearing sandals, white shorts, and a light-blue T-shirt, her red hair tied at the back and hanging past her shoulders—pulled a bottle of diet Coke from her pack. "I can't stand coffee. I don't know how you people drink it, especially first thing in the morning."

"Just one of the many vices of the older generation. How was your summer?" Elkins asked.

"It was okay. I visited my parents. It was good to see them, but a month in Ames is...." She let the sentence trail off and flopped her hand open and out to complete her meaning. "Then I came back here and finished an incomplete from spring term. How about you?"

"I was here most of the summer. I took two weeks off to spend some time with family and some old friends."

"Where?"

"Northern Michigan, God's country. So what brings the News Editor of the *Daily* here so early in the term?"

"Well, first, News Editor was last year; this year I'm Editor-in-Chief. And obviously the big story is the death of Professor Bensen. We'll resume publication on Monday and that will be front page, even though it's week-old news. She was a leading figure in the women's movement on campus, and there was a lot of unhappiness last year with how she was treated by the university. You know, the tenure thing and all." She paused, her tone changed. "I've only got bits and pieces of what happened. What can you tell me?"

"It looks like a suicide," said Elkins. "We're being very thorough with our investigation, and at this time we have no evidence that it is anything else."

"You've always been honest with me, not like Chancellor Pearson, and I know you'll do a very professional job. But regardless of the evidence, you know a lot of people are saying that she must have been murdered. Some of the more wacko radical feminists contend that her death was ordered by the administration and carried out by the university police. There're many crazies out there, lots of anger, hatred, and suspicion."

"How are you going to report it?" asked Elkins.

"I've drafted an article. Will you take a look at it and tell me what you think?"

"Sure. Do you have it with you?"

Reda pulled a sheet from her pack and handed it across the table. "That's a mock-up of the front page."

Elkins read the article.

Controversial Campus Figure Dies.
Foul Play Not Ruled Out.

Sheila Bensen, a popular and controversial member of the English Department for the last seven years, was killed Tuesday morning in a fall from the Patriots' Memorial Carillon.

Although foul play has not been ruled out, police currently believe that the cause of death was suicide

Professor Bensen was a leader in women's issues on campus and in the community for many years. Her activities on behalf of women and the minorities have often angered the university's male-dominated power structure.

Last June the board of governors upheld the university's decision to deny tenure to Professor Bensen. Observers of the campus political scene feel the board's action was a signal that they would continue to support the reactionary policies of Chancellor Pearson's administration.

Brian Battleson, leader of Students for Social and Political Justice (SSPJ), was quoted after the June meeting as saying,

"This was the board giving permission to Pearson to continue the oppression of women and racial and sexual minorities. This university and this state have a long history of supporting the forces of repression. This is one more example of these forces winning out."

Sherry Tompkins, President of Sisters for a Shared Future (SSF), opined at the same time that the denial of tenure was a clear indication that the glass ceiling is alive and well, and if you buck the system you will get pushed out of the university.

English chair, Professor Clifford Chesterton, told Daily reporters that Professor Benson had made major contributions to the Department. Among these contributions he listed two new department offerings, Twentieth Century Women's Literature and Feminist Critical Theory. Further, he noted that although the department had voted not to tenure Professor Benson, her wit, intellect, and bright smile would be missed. Professor Chesterton gave the board the English department's recommendation that she not be tenured.

by Reda Rudd

After he finished, he asked, "Am I just proofreading or do you want me to comment on content?"

"Content, of course, but I'm always happy to have the proofreading, too."

"I'm not comfortable about the foul play line in the headline, although you handle that in the second paragraph, and most of your quotes are inflammatory. I think this sets the tone for your stewardship as editor," he said with a smile.

"Don't be so damn sarcastic. Do you know how hard it is to get undergraduates to think about anything but beer, football, and sex? Besides, a little controversy early in the year sells lots of annual subscriptions."

"I like the article. Especially the fact that I'm not quoted. Pearson would demand to know why I talked to a reporter from the *Daily*."

"See," said Reda, "we're considerate of our friends. Besides, you'll be back to faculty next week."

"I wish that were true. My replacement bailed out, and none of the other candidates were acceptable, so Pearson has formed a new search committee. Looks like I'm stuck with this for most or all of the fall semester."

"Good," retorted Reda in almost a cackle, "for once there will be a good relationship between the university police and the press."

"Well, terrific," Ray said as he rolled his eyes. "While you're here, can you answer some of my questions about Bensen? How well did you know her?"

"Not well. I was in one of her feminist lit courses, and I saw her at the women's movement activities that I was covering or participating in."

"What can you tell me?"

"About?" asked Reda.

"Let's start with the teaching."

"She wasn't a great teacher. I was really interested in the topic, got an 'A' in the class, but she wasn't very good. It's not that she wasn't bright or didn't know the material, but she was never prepared, totally disorganized, and always winging it. When you handed in a paper, you were lucky to ever get it back."

"How did she deal with students?"

"Didn't like men, that's for sure. There were two guys in the feminist lit class, I knew one of them quite well, good student, nice person. They both dropped because she treated them like crap. "

"Example?"

"Her view—everything wrong with the world was because of men. It was a kind of craziness. She linked it to testosterone, which she referred to as 'more deadly than crack.' If you could get past the loony tunes, she had some interesting things to say. She made me aware of writers I hadn't heard of, authors I learned to like. So I'm thankful for that."

"Outside of class, in women's groups?"

"Well, she wasn't the voice of reason. Her positions weren't too radical. They were just irrational. If someone disagreed with her, she would accuse her of being co-opted by the male -dominated society. You can never have a discussion with a person like that. It's like talking to a Bircher."

"How did people, let me rephrase, how did women react to her?"

"They were sort of in a double bind. She was at every meeting, was always there to help with any cause, but was strident and often disruptive. You know what I'm saying?"

"You're saying that people are glad to have someone who is supportive and works for the cause, but at times that help may come at too high of a cost."

"That's right. Let me go back to the article. I'm not asking for your approval, but is it accurate as to the facts surrounding her death?"

"Yes. Again, I'm bothered a bit by the headline on foul play. There is no evidence to support that. On the other hand—I can even give you the appropriate verbiage here, I went to one of those 'writing across the curriculum' workshops last year—you have a good sense of audience and you have provided your reader with enough background information that they know about Bensen and the events leading up to her death."

"You are," said Reda laughingly, "learning the lingo of the biz, the parlance of the palace, and all that good shit." Her tone changed from playful to serious. "You really helped me last year with the dope and date-rape articles. I trust you. If this develops into anything, I hope we can work together." Reda didn't wait for a response. She climbed out of her chair and gave Elkins a high five before she departed.

Elkins sat and watched her go down the hall. He had always loved red hair. His first love, a girl in his third grade class, had red hair. And he had always liked white shorts on a shapely woman.

12

Elkins sat on the deck and looked out at the fields behind his house. The shadows from the trees in the yard were growing longer as the sun slowly slipped away. He sipped on a glass of ginger ale as he read an article from last week's *New Yorker*.

He took another sip, set the glass down, and looked at it. He worried about drinking, not that it had ever caused any problems in his life. He was aware of the fact that in the last year he had been drinking more, and he had moved from wine to Scotch, but usually never more than a drink or two. His father had died from the long-term effects of alcoholism in his fifties.

Since Ellen's death he had developed a pattern of working late and then coming home, preparing dinner, usually frozen dinners warmed in the microwave, having a few drinks, and reading in bed until he fell asleep. The two of them had shared an active social life, attending concerts and plays and going to dinner with friends. Since her death he had become much more isolated.

Elkins looked around at the deck. Ellen had loved it. She had designed it, and he had built it for her—that was a number of years ago, soon after they bought the house. From early spring to late fall she had insisted on having dinner there if the temperature was even close to tolerable. He used to joke about having dinner in a down jacket. Those were happy times. They would cook together, eat, and tell each other about their day.

Evenings were now lonely. The house didn't feel like his anymore, it was more like a motel room. There wasn't the personal connection. The dwelling was still filled with the furnishings that they had collected together, but somehow that connection was gone.

He returned to the kitchen and opened another can of soda, then walked into the living room, turned on the stereo, switched on the deck speakers, and put in a disc. The opening movement of the Tchaikovsky piano trio in A minor was under way by the time he got back to the deck. He set the can on the table and looked at his hands, spreading his fingers like a pianist. He wished he had studied music as a child or teenager. The ability to play an instrument would be a comfort now, but he had come to it too late and with too little talent.

"Drinking alone, that's a bad sign."

Elkins jumped at the sound of the voice.

"Didn't mean to frighten you," said Stephanie Chesterton as she climbed onto the deck.

"I was lost in thought, didn't hear you coming."

"Are you going to get me a drink, or do I have to get my own?"

"What would you like?"

"What are you drinking?"

"Ginger ale."

"Taking the cure, huh? You both had a bit too much to drink the other night."

"Well, if I had stopped with the Scotch, but the wine with dinner...."

"Two bottles of a good Bordeaux."

"I wasn't counting, probably didn't want to know, and then the cognac. That was the coups de grâce. How did Clifford do?"

"He was scheduled to meet with the provost at 9:00 A.M. I played the role of the good wife and called the provost's secretary about 8:45 to say that poor Clifford picked up some horrible intestinal bug and had been up all night. I didn't get too graphic, just enough to suggest that you didn't want to get near him while he was contagious."

"So did he go in to the office?"

"He took a sick day, worked from home, and spent most of the afternoon napping. Any more ginger ale?" asked Stephanie, pushing open the screen door.

"There's a twelve pack in the refrigerator."

A few minutes later Stephanie settled across the table from Ray. She popped the top of the can and slowly poured the soda into a glass.

"So where is Clifford?" asked Ray as he looked across at her. She was wearing a chambray shirt that she had buttoned and tied in a way that covered her while still showing a lot of cleavage. He was attracted to her, had always been, but his commitment to Ellen had always helped him keep his interest in check. Now there was a new reality. It was one more thing he was struggling with, being attracted to women and not knowing how to deal with the attendant emotions. And in the case of Stephanie, the wife of a neighbor and a friend, his feelings were even more uncertain.

"He went over to the pool to swim lengths, and then he planned to sit in the sauna. He has a theory that it takes a couple of days to boil the poison out of your system." She paused and looked closely at Ray, then shifted her gaze away, toward the tall corn stalks in the field beyond the subdivision. "I'm worried about Clifford. He's quite devastated by Bensen's suicide."

"How so?"

"I don't quite know, but he wonders if he should have tried to mentor Bensen during her early years in the department. He said by the time she was on his radar her future in the department was sealed."

"That's sort of silly. She was a professional, his plate is more than full."

"I know," she said looking back at Ray. "Clifford is so damn noble, he thinks he can fix everything, and he's burning out. The Bensen suicide may be the proverbial last straw."

Ray held her gaze.

"Sheila made his life miserable for the last several years. She was constantly creating chaos. Last year he was deposed several times by her lawyers. They intimated in their questioning that he had...."

"I went through a wrongful dismissal suit a few years ago. I know the dance."

"Yes, you don't end up liking lawyers much. And then there are the other problems. The new chancellor is doing his best to defund the humanities, the department has more than it's share of loonies, and Clifford is getting older. He's still struggling with some health issues. I think he's just had it with this job, the university, the town...."

"Are you two...."

"I don't know. We had ten good years. It was a rich time. We travelled to interesting places, were passionate lovers, and wonderful companions. The difference in our ages didn't seem to matter. Then Clifford got cancer. They didn't give us much hope at first. We went up to Rochester. I think they cured him, but at a cost."

They sat in silence for several minutes, then Ray asked, "Where would you go, what would you do?"

"I don't know. I think we're both afraid that we'll just take our emotional baggage with us. Things are just so damn complex." Stephanie paused, then asked, "Will the Bensen investigation take a lot of time?"

"I don't think so. It's still early, but everything says suicide. I can see how Bensen might have felt that life wasn't worth living." He stopped and looked over at Stephanie. "You have an insider's view of the English department. Are there people who might...?"

"Have a motive, no. Sheila was impossible. She was full of anger, full of hate, a master at extracting guilt and often extremely unpleasant. But you don't kill someone for that. Besides, in the English department they are all talk and no action."

Elkins pressed, "You can't think of anyone?"

"No, especially now. Sheila was no longer a threat. Once you're out of the tenure race, you're a non-person, a leper. People just wanted her to go away."

"You're talking about professional things. How about personal relationships?"

"I don't know everything that happens in the department, but I don't think so. She had no love interest there. She wasn't stealing a husband—or wife—as far as I know. No, I don't think there was enough passion on anyone's part to do her in."

"Tuesday night, I don't know if I thanked you. Dinner was wonderful. Hard to be vegetarian when I'm tempted with roast lamb."

She stood up as if she was going to leave and then approached him, bent over and gave him a wet kiss. She knew he had to be looking at her breasts.

"You're more of a carnivore than you realize," she said playfully. "Remember the party Saturday night."

"I thought you probably cancelled it."

"We had the caterer, the food was ordered, and no one was saying we shouldn't have the party. Quite the opposite. Like I said, in her colleagues' eyes, Sheila was a non-person long before she jumped from the carillon."

13

Friday afternoon a few minutes before 2:00 P.M., Ray and Char Pascoe were standing outside of the Campus Interfaith Chapel. "Strange, I walked by this building hundreds of times during my years here and didn't ever quite notice what this place was."

"So you were never inside?" asked Ray.

"Not once. Why are they doing this?"

"Chesterton told me it's something one of Pearson's PR people dreamed up. Having Bensen kill herself, especially in such a public way, doesn't look good for the university. From the beginning of her tenure fight, some of the campus women's groups contended that the administration was trying to unload her because of her political activities. So this is the school's attempt to say that the university really cared."

She laughed, "Would I be too cynical to suggest that if this isn't pure hypocrisy, it is, at least, bad taste?"

"No cynicism on your part. You've demonstrated the rare ability to perceive the obvious with great clarity. But even when you were an undergraduate, I saw that."

"You're almost funny, and I used to think you were just one more boring middle-aged...."

"Careful."

"But, why am I here?" Pascoe asked. "I hate funerals, I'm not much of a church person and...."

"And now you're an adult, an employee, a member of the university community. As part of your initiation, you have to learn about the way we bury our dead. And seriously, we're here gathering data. I want to see who's here, what they say, how they act. Look at it as just part of the job."

Elkins and Pascoe slipped into a side door of the chapel—a splendid example of 60s ugliness—bad design and a strange mix of materials: thin blond bricks, field stone, redwood, copper, brushed aluminum, and weathered shake shingles. The stained glass windows were abstract representations with religious motifs. A small sign under each window contained the artist's interpretation of the work.

The lobby was jammed; Elkins and Pascoe skirted the crowd and got seats in the back, just off the side aisle. A large electric organ in the front, three steps up and on the far right of the nave, flooded the church with Bach. The woman at the keyboard—amply filling a large robe, her bleached blond hair in a beehive—played in a style that was more athletic than aesthetic.

"What's the deal with the music?" asked Pascoe. "Where did they get the organist, a roller-rink?"

"Times are tough in Branson."

Promptly at 3:00, the ushers urged the crowd in, the chapel filled from back to front. The organist launched into the *Kyrie* and *Dies Irae* from Mozart's Requiem, played in swing time.

Elkins pointed to the crucifix above the altar. A pained looking Christ in bleached wood sagged from a large, hammered, copper cross. "Look to the left," he whispered and motioned toward a Star of David and a small Crescent Moon and Star in a dull aluminum, hanging low on the wall. "Who says the university's administration doesn't recognize diversity?"

The organist moved into the opening of the Brahms Academic Overture. Chesterton and Dean Bertram Bateson, in full academic regalia, led the procession up the center aisle. They were closely followed by Father Bob, Chancellor Pearson, and several dozen more faculty members in robes and academic hoods.

Pascoe asked, "What the hell's going on?"

"The dress or the music?"

"Both, either."

"Well, they usually only get to wear that stuff twice a year at graduation. I'm sure they're delighted to have another chance. The choice of music, that's academic." He gestured, turning his hand over and opening his palm with a "what the hell did you expect?" look on his face.

"Who are all these people?"

"Deans, regents, faculty members, anyone who likes to dress up and strut, especially those who enjoy mourning in public. I'm sure we have our share of death followers here, also."

After the procession was seated in the front, a young woman in her late twenties or early thirties, mounted the pulpit. Her glued-on smile gave her a slightly crazed looked. She stood and peered at the congregation for more than a minute holding the painful smile.

"Who's that?" Pascoe asked.

"That's our official chaplain, Patsy Lynn Jolly. Pretty liberal of the administration to have a woman represent the university in celestial affairs."

She began, "I bring you greetings from Jesus Christ and the Kingdom of God. And I have great news, wonderful news, terrific news. Sheila Bensen is with him. Our dear friend and colleague is now beyond the pain and suffering of this world. Sheila is now in eternal joy."

Patsy Lynn rambled on for quite some time. The congregation became increasingly restless. Finally, she asked the congregation to stand and join her in reciting the Lord's Prayer. Elkins looked around to see who was participating.

Chesterton spoke next. Standing high over the congregation, he began, his rich voice booming out at the audience.

"From medieval times, the university has been a community of scholars, an order committed to the pursuit of truth and the preservation of knowledge. We share the joys of discovery, and the pleasures of scholarly accomplishment, and we take pride in passing our collected knowledge from generation to generation. But like all communities, we also share sadness and loss, so it is that today we gather to mourn the passing of our esteemed colleague, Professor Sheila Bensen, a remarkable woman and a dedicated teacher. She understood a scholar's obligation to the needs of...."

"Fucking hypocrite," came a loud whisper.

Elkins looked in vain for the source.

"....and her many contributions will be remembered and honored. Her work will remain part of the rich legacy of this university. We celebrate her life. We mourn her passing."

Father Bob followed Chesterton. "We are gathered here today to remember Sheila Bensen. She was a remarkable woman and committed and caring teacher, and in her own unique way, a devoted Catholic...."

Father Bob's comments were very brief. Then he invited members of the congregation to come forward and say a few words about Benson. At least a dozen did; all but one were female. The one male, a tall gangly kid with orange hair, told the congregation how Bensen changed his life by taking him out of this century and connecting him with the past. The others, serious looking women, talked about Bensen's commitment to the women's movement and to social justice. Elkins noted that their sincerity and passion was more compelling than the earlier remarks.

The service concluded with a young woman, backed by guitars, singing "Amazing Grace," slightly off key and with a Nashville twang. The organist pounded some up-tempo Bach for the recessional. Elkins and Pascoe slipped out a side door.

"What now?" asked Pascoe.

"There will be a reception at the University Club. Sherry, small sandwiches, cheese and crackers, a silver tray with chocolates, and polite conversation."

"Are we going to take this in, too?"

"I've got some other things I've got to get done. You can go if you want to."

"No thanks. Let me ask you this. What did you learn or see there, anything significant?"

Elkins smiled at her. "You don't usually have an 'aha' experience when you're confronted with new knowledge, the 'aha' comes later when you've had an opportunity to integrate it with everything else you know. That's when you make the cognitive leap."

"And when is that going to happen?"

"You can never tell. Sometimes it's at 3:00 A.M. Some times when you're in the shower, or walking, or driving. You've just got to let things percolate."

"Aha," said Pascoe.

14

Ray spent Saturday in his office doing catch-up on the paperwork. It was the kind of task he hated. First he had to review and sign several dozen purchase orders. Then he read through and approved leave requests. And last he had to respond to dozens of memos, most coming via e-mail, many requiring a carefully written response. Without the interruptions of the normal workday, Ray was able to complete most of the work that had piled up as his attention had been directed at the investigation of the death of Sheila Bensen.It was early evening by the time he returned home. He settled on his deck with a microwave dinner and the *Times*, the sun low on the horizon. The sound of voices in the Chesterton's yard indicated that the English Department party was already in full swing.

Ray was almost through the Op Ed section when he was startled by Stephanie's sudden appearance out of the shadows.

"Are you coming over, or are you just going to sit here?"

"I thought maybe I'd sit here. I'm awfully tired and not feeling very social."

"Come on Elkins, you've got to stop this. You can't become a hermit. You've got to get on with your life."

"I'd have to shower and shave and...."

"You look fine. If you want, you can throw on a sport coat, but even that isn't necessary. You know how the men in the English department dress. Half of them won't wear a coat. Come on." Stephanie was behind his chair, pulling it back from the table and herding him into the house.

"I'll get you a coat." She disappeared into the house. Stephanie had been Ellen's best friend and knew Elkins's house almost as well as her own. He could visualize her marching into the bedroom, opening the walk-in closet, and looking through his sport coats, quickly rejecting most of them.

She reappeared with a blue, lightweight blazer.

Ray looked at it. "That's fairly wrinkled."

"It's the best there is. Everything in there should be sent to the cleaners." Pulling the coat off the hanger she said,

"Come on Elkins. You'll look terrific in it." She helped him into the jacket, then stood in front of him and straightened the collar. She kissed him, full on the mouth. "You're a good man, Ray. Good men shouldn't be wasted." Taking him by the hand, she led him out of the house and across the lawn to her house. They pushed their way into the living room.

"What do you want?" she asked.

"Scotch."

Ray watched her fight to the bar. When she got back, she handed him two glasses and said, "Thought I better get you a couple of drinks while I was there."

Elkins sipped one of the drinks. "This tastes like straight Scotch."

"Shouldn't ruin it with water. Besides, you're behind the rest."

Stephanie got a look of delight as she surveyed the crowd. "This party is something. Everyone comes, gets drunk, and forgets that they hate each other. I love seeing Clifford's distinguished colleagues get all cleaned up and then act like a bunch of animals. Free food and booze makes them crazy."

She pointed to two waiters, one clearing the way, the other carrying a large punch bowl filled with shrimp. Before they got to the serving table, people were reaching over and around one another, picking handfuls from the bowl. Eventually the waiters set the bowl on the table, but their retreat was made difficult because the crowd surged forward to snatch the last remnants from the bowl. "Note the blood frenzy," continued Stephanie. "It's common to sharks, piranhas, grizzly bears in heat, and down-at-the-heels humanities professors."

"It's quite astonishing."

"The first few years I found this embarrassing, but now I'm amused."

Reda Rudd slid her arm through Elkins's and playfully bumped a hip against his. He noted that her party uniform was a far cry from her undergraduate, activist/editor garb. The Birkenstocks, T-shirt, and shorts had been replaced by a more sophisticated persona, chic and tailored. The Scotch was starting to hit. Elkins looked at the fashionable Reda, seeing her in a different way.

The sensation passed. Reda seemed to be with someone, older then her, but still quite young. She introduced the man, Gus Ginopolis, as a member of the English department. Over the noise he picked up bits and pieces of the conversation.

Stephanie liberated him from the triangle. With charm and skill she led him toward the kitchen. She was stopped along the way by a man who, in Italian, launched into a long, highly-animated speech; he was tall, thin, African-black, with James Baldwin eyes and hands that moved with each inflection. Stephanie rattled back in Italian; she smiled, but Elkins sensed that she was trying to extricate herself. She pulled someone new into the conversation, a woman—short, round, wrapped in brightly painted material, face layered with powder, chopsticks jutting from a gray-black bun. Once they'd started talking, she pulled Elkins away. He passed his drinks to a waiter.

From the kitchen, she guided him through the basement door. As they went down the steps Elkins asked, "Who were those people?

"Faculty. The woman's Bobby Jo Hendrickson," Stephanie replied.

Who was that man speaking Italian?"

"That was Seneca Carducci."

"What does he do?"

She paused at the base of the steps and turned to him; she put her arms around his neck and leaned into him. "His dissertation was on the writers of the Harlem Renaissance. He was hired to expand an Afro-American lit program. But a few years after he got here he had a Fulbright in Italy. There he discovered—don't ask me how—that his true ethnic heritage was Italian. When he came back he changed his name and refused to teach any more Black lit courses, saying he was being discriminated against. Now he says he's a Dante and Nabokov specialist."

"Interesting combination. And the Italian?"

"When he's had a few drinks, he loses his capacity to speak English. He says that was the final proof—in his last life he was in Renaissance Italy. He's sure he was a Medici. Always wears those black suits. The man is very taken with Italian gangsters—Italy, not Chicago. I know this all sounds crazy—being slightly drunk makes it more plausible."

"No," Elkins shook his head.

Stephanie opened a heavy door, pulled him forward and pushed it shut behind them. She turned off the lights. He saw rows of bottles on racks before the room went black. He felt her opening his shirt and running her hands over his chest. She pulled away from him, and then he felt her naked breasts, her tongue slowly sliding back and forth between his lips.

She pulled away. A few seconds later the lights went on and she was dressed, looking unruffled. He reached for her, but she moved beyond his grasp. Then she turned and buttoned his shirt.

"You have a nice chest," she taunted.

"So do you." Then the anger hit. "What the hell are you doing? This isn't fair to me, it isn't fair to...."

"Isn't fair to whom...to Clifford? You know about us, he doesn't care. To Ellen, she's dead, Elkins. It's been a year. You want me, and you don't know how to deal with it."

"But this kind of teasing..."

"I want to tease you. I want you to get angry. I haven't seen any affect for months. I'm going to push you until I know you're alive again." She playfully slapped him a few times, two hands, one on each cheek.

She grabbed his hand and pulled him along, turned and kissed him quickly at the top of the steps, and then said, "Come on, there's someone I want to introduce you to."

She guided him through the chaos, moving toward a group in the living room and extracted a woman—petite, attractive—from the group. Stephanie introduced them. "Jane, this is Ray Elkins, the man I told you about. Elkins, this is Jane Arden." Stephanie tried to get a conversation going, but was pulled away by a member of the catering staff.

After a few minutes of trying to talk over the noise, Jane suggested they go out and get some air. She led the way toward the front door. They paused and looked into the library. Chesterton was holding court, a circle of junior faculty members hanging on every word.

They found the smokers in the front yard, clustered in small groups. Reda Rudd was standing off to the side with Father Bob. She motioned them over. Elkins noticed how she was standing, suggesting an intimacy between them that he wouldn't have expected.

"Do you...." she gestured toward Father Bob.

"Yes, we've met." They shook hands.

Elkins started to introduce Arden. She cut him off. "We're all acquainted. Nice to see you again," she said as she shook hands with Reda. "I've enjoyed reading your pieces in the *Daily.*"

Reda turned to Elkins. "Is there anything new...."

Her question was cut off by a long horn blast from an eighteen-wheeler, the scream of rubber against cement, the report of metal against metal and exploding glass. As they turned in the direction of the sound, a small tongue of yellow flame began to illuminate the wreckage. Ray ran toward the entrance of the subdivision.

The scene was lit by the yellow flames. The crushed remnants of a small car were just behind the tractor wheels of a large truck. Burning fuel poured across the road into a ditch. A man in tan work clothes, his face lit by the flames, stood looking at the wreckage.

"Are you hurt?" asked Elkins

"There was nothing I could do. It ran the stop sign," he yelled. The car was now a pillar of fire, there was no sign of its occupant.

Lights flashing, siren screaming, a sheriff's car braked hard and came to a halt, headlights on the wreck. The deputy climbed out, pulled an extinguisher from his trunk, and emptied it on the blaze. Then the first fire engine rumbled to a stop. The crew, in full protective gear, jumped from the rig and deployed hoses, covered the burning vehicles with foam, the spotlights from their truck reflecting off their heavy coats, helmets, and facemasks. Several more emergency vehicles arrived on the scene before the fire was completely under control. Minutes ticked past and things started to slow down again. Ray kept hearing the name Bobby Jo Hendrickson repeated in the crowd of spectators that had formed behind him.

He gave his name as a witness to the accident to one of the deputies, and then walked through the crowd and in the direction of his house. The air was heavy with the smell of burning rubber, plastic, oil, gasoline, and flesh.

Later, as he was standing in the shower, trying to wash the stink of the fire from his body, he remembered Jane Arden. He had left her standing on the lawn with Reda Rudd and Father Bob. He wondered if he would ever see her again.

15

On Monday, Labor Day, Ray was in the office from mid-morning until late afternoon. On his way home he stopped at the health food store near central campus and picked up some fresh bread, two soft avocados, a lime, and some alfalfa sprouts in a plastic, cube-shaped container.

He laid out the ingredients on a cutting board. First, he quartered the lime, squeezed one of the quarters into a tall glass, added ice, and filled it to the top with quinine water. Then he halved both of the avocados, cutting to the pit and twisting the halves, one in each hand, until they came apart. He scraped the flesh away from the skin into a stainless steel mixing bowl. He squeezed lime juice from the remaining three quarters over the avocado. With a whisk, he mashed the pulp, mixing in the lime juice. Tasting the mixture with each addition, he sprinkled in salt, and garlic powder. The concluding touch was seven shakes of Frank's Hot Sauce.

Using a serrated knife, he lopped the heel off the loaf, and then cut two thick slices, noting with satisfaction the thick crust. He spread part of the avocado mixture on one slice, added a layer of alfalfa sprouts and the second slice, and then cut the sandwich on the diagonal.

As Ray stood over the sink and ate the sandwich, he was startled by the sound of the door to the deck sliding open.

Stephanie stepped in. "What are you doing?"

"Dinner."

"You should come over, we still have tons of leftovers. The accident brought the party to an end. You didn't come back."

"I went home. Didn't feel like being social anymore."

"But you must have seen that kind of thing before."

"Too many times. I don't need to do it again."

"It's Ellen, isn't it?"

"I don't know."

"You've never really dealt with death before, have you? I mean, the death of someone you're close to, someone you loved."

"My father died a few years ago," he offered.

"Important, but not the same. Your grief was not the same as your mother's."

Ray nodded.

"Do you know what you need?" she asked.

"What?"

"You need a woman."

He reddened. Stephanie could feel his anger.

"Don't say anything." She cut him off before he could start. She knew what he was going to say. "I know how much you still hurt, and I know that you think this is too simple of a solution. But you're never going to get through your grief if you don't start seeing people. "

Elkins made a sweeping motion with his hand in her direction. "We're not alike."

"True. You find me a bit outrageous, you might even think I'm a bit of a tramp, or you feel sorry for Clifford. Don't. He's a realist, and so am I. If he could be my lover, I wouldn't be out there. He understands me and my needs. Other than sex, we have a workable marriage, more than most people." She moved closer to him.

"Ray, you can take a lover without feeling guilty, and maybe it would get you back with the living."

"When did you become my self-appointed...."

"We've known each other a long time. You're bright and funny and a joy to be with, but since Ellen's illness I've watched you pull in, and I don't see signs you're making any attempt to come out. I've appointed myself to kick you in the ass because I can't stand extended grief and self-pity. What are you drinking?"

"Tonic water, diet tonic water."

"Gin?"

"No, just tonic water."

"Got any?"

Elkins pointed to the cabinet that held the liquor.

As Stephanie rifled through the bottles, he asked, "You want a sandwich?"

"What is it?"

"Avocado and sprouts on whole wheat."

"God, you buy cheap gin," she said as she started making a drink. "I see why you're sticking with the tonic." She reached around him, pulled a tumbler from a shelf and splashed in some soda. "Sure you don't want to come over for leftovers?"

"No, I'm happy with this. Where's Clifford?"

"He's at the office trying to get the schedule covered. He's moving people around, trying to cover the classes that had been assigned to Hendrickson and Bensen. Then he's got to hire adjuncts to teach uncovered sections. And this has all got to happen by tomorrow morning when classes start." She paused, "You're cleverly changing the subject. You need a woman."

"Are you offering yourself, selflessly, in an attempt to save me?"

She looked coy. "I've always found you attractive, but I kept my hands off you because of Ellen. Plus, I don't think it's good to have lovers in the neighborhood. That said, I'm available, but if it's not me, it should be someone."

"You're a regular Mother Teresa, aren't you?"

"Okay, be a bastard about it. Spend your time working and sleeping. It's your life you're wasting."

Elkins watched her leave, carrying her drink with her. He wished she had stayed.

16

<hr>

Early in the workday on Tuesday morning, Ray gingerly carried two large cups of coffee and a bag from the Boulangerie André from the parking lot into the medical center. With his precious load, he carefully negotiated the revolving door, took the elevator to the subway level, and made his way to the pathology department.

Dr. Gutiérrez turned away from her computer screen and looked at him.

"It's a good thing I come in early. In most places you would have to wait a day or two for this." She motioned to the screen. "This wasn't in your jurisdiction, was it?"

"No, but I was at the scene. I'm interested in the case."

Gutiérrez pointed at the bag.

"Coffee," Elkins responded. "Coffee and dark chocolate croissants."

"Good. The autopsy put me behind schedule. I'm an hour late for my morning snack. You joining me?"

"I'll just stick with the coffee."

Gutiérrez looked in the bag. "You better eat one, doctor's orders."

"Why?"

"Because I don't want to get fat."

"Aren't you still refereeing youth soccer?"

"Yes, running my butt off trying to keep up with the kids. And what I'm trying to tell you is that I don't need any extra butt. So eat, you're looking undernourished."

Gutiérrez placed the croissants on some paper plates she pulled from a bottom desk drawer and passed Ray a paper towel to use as a napkin.

"These are great, Ray," she said after consuming half of the pastry. "Now if we could get a decent bagel without having to go a thousand miles. Can we talk about the accident without ruining your appetite?"

"Sure," said Ray.

"What exactly happened?"

"It looked like the Hendrickson ran a stop sign and slammed into the side of a truck. There was a fire. It was horrible. I left when things appeared to be under control. It was more than I could deal with."

"Well, the victim was a bit broasted, but the body was pretty much intact. Maybe you couldn't see it. The victim was decapitated. Probably never knew what hit her, or I guess in this case what she hit. Head's in good shape. I talked to one of the EMT's this morning who was at the scene."

"Yes?"

"He told me when they removed the body, they couldn't find the head. They looked around the accident scene, even in the ditches by the side of the road. Finally he found it on the floor of the passenger's side, way at the front under the dash. Said it was sort of weird, head was down there and so was a bourbon bottle." She looked up and gave Ray an amused smile. "Her blood alcohol was 0.23. Glad it didn't boil off. We wouldn't have been able to determine that," she laughed at her joke. "So what's your interest in this?"

"The accident was at the entrance to my sub. I was at the same party. I may have even been introduced to the woman. You know what it's like at a noisy party."

"Yes, been there. People talking at one another, but you're often just guessing at what's being said."

"Here's what's special," said Ray. "This is the second member of the English department to die in a week. At that blood alcohol level, what did you say, 0.23, how well could she function?"

"It depends, most of us wouldn't be able to walk, but someone who is habituated to alcohol, they can handle it. During my internship I'd see people in the ER with this level or even higher, and you'd hardly know that they had been drinking. The human body is an amazing machine. It can adapt to almost any abuse, at least for a while. This woman, what's her name?" She glanced at the screen. "Hendrickson, you can tell she was a hard drinker, had been for years." She gestured with the pastry. "These are great, thank you."

Elkins nodded.

"It's the only place in town where you can get decent pastries or bread. Most of these flat-landers don't understand baking. Their palettes have never gotten beyond Little Debbie." She ate the last bit of the croissant, and then licked the chocolate off her fingers. "Who's going to identify the body? Does she have family locally?"

"I don't think so."

"Well, this isn't a job for the squeamish."

"I'll ask the department chair. He identified Bensen."

"This one looks better than Bensen. Hairs a bit singed and one ear is rather crisp, and she has sort of a detached look on her face, if you know what I mean." She gave Elkins a naughty-child grin. "You know what I'm really sorry about? That I encouraged you to eat the other croissant. But before you go..."

"Yes," said Ray.

Gutiérrez pulled a blood pressure cuff and stethoscope from a file drawer. "Let's do right arm, then left arm, and average the two."

Ray submitted, knowing that a lecture would follow.

17

~~~~~~~~

Reda Rudd stood at Ray's office door. He waved her in. "Have a seat. Are you okay?"

"I guess I wanted to ask you the same thing. I saw you wander away sometime after the fire trucks arrived. I looked for you later and couldn't find you."

"I went home. It was all too much," Ray said.

"That's surprising. I assumed you had dealt with things like that when you were a cop. What did you tell me, Detroit?"

"Good memory. And I did see my share of death and mayhem. And at the time I coped with it. I think I may have had better defenses then. I was just doing a job, being a professional." Elkins sat and rocked a bit in his chair.

"And now?" asked Reda.

"I don't know. I haven't had to deal with death and violence on a day-to-day basis for years. Perhaps I've lost my professional distance. Or maybe I'm just getting older, becoming increasingly aware of my mortality." He paused and looked thoughtful. "When I saw you in front of Chesterton's house, were you leaving?"

"No, I lost my date, the jerk. I came out to see if he was having a smoke. We'd had a thing about tobacco earlier in the evening. Anyway, I ran into Father Bob while I was looking for Gus."

"How do you know Father Bob?"

"I'm sort of Catholic, or at least my family is. My freshman year I attended Mass from time to time. Haven't seen him much since then." She paused, " A question, that woman you were standing with, Jane Arden, was she your date?"

"No, I had just been introduced to her. We went out for some air. Why do you ask?"

"After the crash, you just left her standing there. To be honest, Elkins, I thought it was sort of peculiar."

Ray visualized the scene. "I really know how to impress a woman, don't I? I should have checked on her later."

"It was a chaotic scene. If you weren't really with her, it's probably no big thing. I had Arden my sophomore year, a survey class. She's a smart woman, nice person, too."

"Did you go back to the party?" asked Ray.

"Yes."

"And?"

"I went to find Gus. I wanted to go home. There were a whole lot of people on the inside who didn't know anything had happened, but it didn't take long for the word to spread. Then things were over rather quickly. Everyone left en masse."

"Did you know Hendrickson?"

"I had her winter term last year for Southern Writers. A wonderful instructor, she had lots of interesting anecdotes about the writers we were studying. She really knew the material and the back-stories of the writers and their works. She gave us the impression that bourbon was a very important part of the creative process for most of these writers."

"Did you know her outside of class?" Ray asked.

"After the final, we went to a bar, most of the class. That was the only time."

"Did you see Hendrickson at the party?"

"I talked to her for a while early in the evening, and I saw her when I was standing with Father Bob. She stopped for a minute and joked with us. She said department parties reminded her of Polish weddings. It seemed funny at the time, but I have no idea what she was talking about."

"How did she seem? Intoxicated?"

"I don't think so. Her speech wasn't slurred, she wasn't staggering or anything."

"Did she leave alone or was anyone with her?"

"She was alone. She waved at me as she walked down the driveway. You came out and then a few minutes later there was that awful crash." Reda assumed her reporter's tone, "We want to do a complete story on the accident. What can you tell...."

Elkins raised his hand to stop her. "You'll have to talk to the Sheriff's Department. They're handling the investigation. You need to get to know the Sheriff, Jack Kackmeister. He's a good guy and a graduate student of mine. I'll tell him that you're a real professional."

"Thanks, Elkins. I owe you. You know, I had to interview Kackmeister last year when I was working on a story. I could hardly get him to say anything. Why are cops so damn paranoid about reporters?"

"You can probably answer that question. First, they have to be careful not to disclose anything that might ruin a possible prosecution. And second, so many cops have been done in by reporters—misquoted or had things taken out of context."

"How about just CYAing?"

"There's that and sometimes incompetence or corruption. You ran into that on your big story last year."

"Yes. That was an education."

"Oh, by the way, your date, a long-term relationship?" asked Ray.

"No, I just met him. I'm still recovering from a love affair that ended very badly."

"So, who is this guy?"

"Gus, he's new to the department, his first year. Got his degree from Northwestern, American Studies. I just met him a few days ago. We live in the same apartment complex. It was our first date, probably the last. I can't stand guys that smoke. Did you ever smoke, Elkins?"

"I did, and I quit. I started again, and I quit. I think I'm beyond it."

"Tobacco, how did you kick it?"

"Getting involved with a woman who hated it. I had to make a choice."

"Good for you. Thanks, Ray."

~~~~~

18

Sharon Anderson watched Ray get off the elevator and walk to the glass door that opened to the Chancellor's office. As he approached her desk, she said, "You can go right in. Please know, he's in a lousy mood." She reached out and briefly held on to his hand.

"What's going on?" Ray asked.

"There've been too many calls from the press. That sets him off every time."

"Thanks for the warning," said Ray. He knocked and waited a few seconds before he turned the handle and went in. Pearson was on the phone.

"The people from media relations will get back to you as soon as we have the complete story. Yes, it's tragic to lose two members of one department, but I can assure you that it's purely coincidental. There is nothing to those reports of discontent in the humanities faculty. That's just pure bunk. People playing politics, nothing more."

Pearson slammed the receiver down. "That's the kind of bullshit I've got to put up with. The *State News* is running an editorial in this afternoon's edition that the two 'suicides' this week in the English department are a symptom of the deteriorating morale in the university's humanities faculty. They just faxed it over." He waved a couple of sheets of paper in Elkins's direction. "He, the editor, wanted a comment from me that they could include in tomorrow's edition. Bastard. So what the hell is going on, anyway?"

"With Hendrickson?"

"Yes, who the hell do you think I'm talking about?"

"As far as I can tell, it was a traffic accident." Ray dropped into a chair across from Pearson. "Hendrickson ran a stop sign and hit a truck. Her blood alcohol was more than 0.23. She was intoxicated."

"Two in one week. You know how these play on the farm. Those good people pay high taxes so a bunch of pointy-headed intellectuals at the state university can run around killing themselves or getting killed. You should go to the legislative hearings and beg for money from those SOBs. If I've heard it once, I've heard it a thousand times. Stories about their kids or the kids of friends and neighbors who come here, God-fearing and with strong family values, and after four years they're nothing but a bunch of fornicating drug addicts and drunks."

"How you gonna keep'em down on the farm after they've seen..."

"What?" asked Pearson.

"Just a line from an old song that seemed to fit. What do you want me to do?"

"Can you get the sheriff to cooperate?"

"He's a graduate and is currently working on a Ph.D. He will help in any way that is proper and legal."

"A sheriff getting a Ph.D. What the hell's the world coming to? Common sense and some muscle used to be enough. Now you got to get a Ph.D. to make up for a lack of it."

Ray was about to interrupt. He kept reminding himself that the war was more important than the battle.

"This is what I want," continued Pearson, "I want a good, clear statement from the sheriff that this was an accident. I don't want the word suicide even hinted at in the statement. Be nice if you could leave alcohol out, too. Can you do that?"

"I can handle the suicide part. I don't know where that came from. There's nothing to suggest this was anything other than an accident. Hendrickson's alcohol level is already public record. You can't change the facts. The sheriff's integrity...."

"Integrity hell, how about my integrity, how about the integrity of this school?

Elkins controlled his anger. "Is there anything else?"

"No. Just get that statement. I want our people to have a press release on this as fast as possible. They can add all the crap about what a wonderful scholar she was and make it look like the usual release when a faculty member dies."

"I will get you an accurate statement of the facts from the sheriff." Ray got up and left the office.

Sharon looked up and smiled, "I told you."

"How do you take it day after day?"

Without hesitation she responded, "Yoga and breathing exercises, that and the positive energy that comes from the knowledge that chancellors come and chancellors go. Take care of yourself, Elkins. Don't let the bad karma rub off." She gave him a warm smile and reached to touch his hand again. Then, "Namaste," she softly offered, placing the tips of her fingers together.

19

Elkins met Sheriff Jack Kackmeister at the county storage yard, a fenced area behind the road commission building.

"As soon as I saw your name as a witness on the accident report, I knew that you would be over to have a look at this."

Elkins gave him a questioning look.

"Since the victim is a faculty member, I knew you'd want to know everything about the accident. Here's the report." He handed a manila folder to Elkins.

After reading the report, Elkins handed the folder back to Kackmeister. "That's a good piece of work, thorough and literate."

"I made sure it was extra clean. I hold our interns to the same standards you held me to as an undergrad. Does the report jibe with your observations?"

"I think that's essentially what happened."

"Where were you at the time of the accident?" Kackmeister asked.

"I was at a party at Clifford Chesterton's. He's the chair of the English department. Do you know him?"

Kackmeister made a negative nod.

"I was standing in the front lawn talking when I heard the crash and ran over. The vehicle was quickly engulfed in flames. One of your road patrol cars was there almost immediately. The fire trucks arrived soon after. I left when they got there. Report says you didn't find any skid marks."

"I went over there yesterday with my accident specialist. There were no skid marks on Wimbledon or Townline Road. It doesn't look like she touched her brakes. The driver of the truck, however, tried to stop, but he was fully loaded. The car is over here." He led Elkins to the burned shell of the Jaguar convertible.

"Any possibility of some kind of mechanical failure?"

"There's too much damage to reach any conclusions. The car is more than twenty years old. Ted, our chief mechanic, looked the wreck over. He said there is always the possibility of a catastrophic failure in the brakes, but even in a car as old as that one there is a lot of redundancy. We'll never know if there was a mechanical problem. I talked with the pathologist who did the autopsy. Hendrickson was 0.23 or greater."

"I know. I talked with Dr. Gutiérrez this morning. Hendrickson was rumored to be a very serious drinker. It's hard to know how well she was functioning. So where does that leave us?"

"Will I be graded on my answer?" Kackmeister asked with a smile.

"No, as long as you get your dissertation done this year."

"Well, we can't rule out mechanical problems, and alcohol was a factor, perhaps the major factor."

Elkins asked, "Who does most of the foreign car service in town?"

"Guy's name is Kimber, Cecil Kimber. His place is on the far west side of town on the highway, Import Auto. It's next to, but sort of tucked behind, the Big Top Truck Stop, small white block building."

"Thanks," said Ray. "There's one more thing. Well, two more. First, Reda Rudd, the editor of the *Daily,* will be calling you. She's been doing a story on Hendrickson's death."

"Last time I dealt with the *Daily*...."

"She's all right, Jack. She's smart, professional, and honest. You don't have to worry about her. She's the one who brought the athletic dorm scandal to light. I told her you'd be happy," Ray emphasized the word 'happy,' "to provide her with your findings at the appropriate time."

"I'll do my best," responded Kackmeister.

Ray noted the lack of enthusiasm in Kackmeister's tone.

"What's the second thing?"

"The Chancellor would like a statement from you on the accident. He's going to have PR people produce a press release that unequivocally states this was an accident. He wants to make sure he has the documentation to back up the claim. Seems the *State News* is running an editorial suggesting this was the second faculty suicide in a week. I think a copy of that report," Ray pointed to the folder, "would be more than adequate. If you would be good enough to fax it over, I'd appreciate it."

"I'll do that. Let me know if there is anything else you need."

"Thanks," said Ray, "How's the dissertation? I haven't seen you lately."

"Lots going on right now. I'll get on it again once the kids are back in school. Fall's a better time for writing."

20

<hr/>

Ray's first task on Wednesday morning was to interview Cecil Kimber. As he approached the cinderblock building, Ray smiled as he noted that the sign "Import Auto" also contained the line "and Sports Cars" in small faded blue letters. He entered through the door marked "Office." Finding no one, he pushed open the door at the rear of the office and walked into the garage, a large open area. Decades of dirt and grime clung to the once white walls and steel framed windows. A few faded and yellowing Snap-on calendars hung at random locations around the dingy interior. Vehicles in various states of disassembly, some on jack stands, littered the opposing sides of the garage, the center a pathway to the large overhead door at the end of the building. The atmosphere was redolent of oil, gasoline, rubber, exhaust fumes, and mineral spirits. Rush Limbaugh ranted from a boom box at the back of a tool-cluttered workbench. Ray saw two mechanics. He approached the first one who was hunched over a Safety-Kleen tank busily scrubbing some parts. As the man looked up from his work, Ray asked, "Kimber?"

"He's out back," the man motioned with his head toward the open garage door at the rear of the building.

Ray could see someone working under the hood of a small sports car. He walked out and approached the car. He looked under the hood from the opposite side. "Problems?"

"Idiot screws up the distributer and then has it towed here because it doesn't start."

"Kimber?"

"That's me. What do you need?" he asked coming up from under the hood. Ray thought he looked mildly familiar, almost cherubic—albeit forty something—rosy cheeks, round face, blue-tinted John Lennon glasses, and a black Greek fisherman's hat. "Information. I was wondering if Bobby Jo Hendrickson had her Jag serviced here?"

"Who's asking?" Kimber's voice suggested apprehension.

"Name's Elkins, University Police."

"We took care of it, solid car. Professor Hendrickson, she was a hell of a nice lady. Made me sick when I saw the picture in the paper."

"Had you done any work on her car lately?"

"Yes, last winter. She only drove it in dry weather, that's why it was so good, part of the reason, anyway. She also spent the money necessary to keep it safe and running good. Students don't do that, and the faculty usually isn't much better, sometimes worse.

"What kind of work did you do on her car?"

"As I was saying, last winter we did the front suspension, new bushings in the kingpins, all the rubber parts, and renewed the shocks."

"Anything else?"

"Bob fitted a new top, pain in the ass job."

"How about the brakes?"

"We did all the hydraulics, rebuilt the calipers, and put in new pads. Replaced the master cylinder. Put in new brake lines and rubber hoses. Everything first class, the way that kind of job should be done. Also did belts and hoses on the engine."

"You do the work?"

"Yes."

"There's not a chance that the brakes might have failed?"

Kimber responded emphatically, "The brakes in that car were as good as when it left the factory. Other than the pads, that system would have been bulletproof for years."

"Could she have hit something that damaged the system?"

"No chance. Everything's protected. To damage a hose, you'd have to tear out the lower wishbone. If she had done that, the car would not have been drivable." Kimber paused, his tone changed. "She was a nice woman. I'll miss her."

"How well did you know her?"

"Not well, but better than most of my customers. University people are strange, but she was different. She was respectful to the guys and me. Appreciated what we did. She never batted an eye about what something cost. Just wanted things done right, you know what I mean.

"Hendrickson always came by about noon on Christmas Eve with a bottle of Scotch, the good stuff. She was a bourbon drinker, but she knew I liked Scotch, so that's what she brought. Last year we sat in my office and drank most of it. I could hardly walk, but booze didn't seem to bother her much. She drove me home."

"I don't know much about mechanics," said Ray, "so I'm going to cover the same ground again. It's not that I don't believe you. I'm just trying to understand what you're telling me. In your professional judgment, there's not a chance the brakes could have failed?"

Kimber looked thoughtful for a minute. "I won't say it's impossible, only a damn fool would say that. But the chances of a total failure would be one in a million."

21

Char Pascoe spread the materials across the surface of Ray's desk. "Here is Hendrickson's HR file, and these are the transcripts of the interviews I conducted with the secretary in the English department and Hendrickson's office mate, Seneca Carducci. What a smart, engaging character he is."

Elkins looked up and smiled, but didn't bother to explain. "I'll read through them in a bit. Have a seat and give me a summary of what you've found."

"Hendrickson was in her sixth year. She came here from Northern Illinois. She did her graduate work at Chapel Hill. Her specialty was medieval literature, but she mostly taught classes on Southern writers. I picked up this book in the English Department." She pulled an 8 ½" by 11" Xeroxed booklet from the pile of documents. "This is published by the Association of English Majors. There's a summary of student evaluations for every professor, including grade distributions and a sampling of comments made about instructors. Hendrickson was very popular."

She continued, "I checked with the Department of Motor Vehicles. There are two autos registered to her. One is a five-year-old Toyota, the second is the Jaguar she was driving the night of the accident. Carducci told me that her father had given her the car years ago when she completed her Ph.D. She only drove it during the summer months.

"According to college HR records, she didn't list a beneficiary on either the retirement or the life insurance the college provides.

She did enter a next of kin on her initial employment application, an aunt. I called the number and got a retirement home in South Carolina. They said they had no one by that name and checked their records. Hendrickson's aunt has been deceased for five years."

"In sum," said Elkins, "she has no living relatives."

Pascoe nodded. "I asked Carducci about her friends, people she might have been involved with in a relationship. He dropped his very European way of speaking and said with a heavy Southern accent, 'Why honey, she took on everyone: white, black, brown, men, women, old, young—didn't seem to matter. Equal opportunity, honey, but no quotas.'" Pascoe started to laugh, then stopped and blushed. Ray chuckled, mostly at her embarrassment.

"Then I talked briefly with Alice Widdowson, Chesterton's secretary. Do you know her?"

"I've met her a couple of times, and I've talked to her on the phone. Seems professional and competent. But sort of a tyrant type."

"I'm sure she is. She told me that Hendrickson was a popular teacher, but—and I wish I could duplicate her tone—she said that Hendrickson wasn't in control of her life. When I asked her to explain, she told me that Hendrickson never followed departmental procedures and didn't do things like returning the Xerox key to the correct place in the office. Widdowson continued on with a whole litany of things: every semester Hendrickson was always the last faculty member to turn in her grades, she seldom attended department meetings, and she never picked up her mail." Pascoe smiled, "I think it's real easy to get on Widdowson's wrong side."

"Apparently. Anything else?" asked Elkins.

"Couple. Widdowson, when I asked if she knew anything about Hendrickson's personal life, said that she had heard, and these are her words, that Hendrickson was a 'shameless libertine.' I really love the phrase. It's something my great aunt, who is ninety-three, might say."

"Rather strong language," he responded with a smile.

"Also," continued Pascoe, "Carducci told me that Hendrickson wasn't a drunk, but she did like her bourbon. He said something like 'devoted to her bourbon.' I checked her driving records. She's had two DUIs, one last year and one five years ago. She also had a speeding ticket several years ago. Nothing else. I wish I had majored in English as an undergrad."

"Why's that?" asked Ray.

"These people are so interesting and live such exotic lives compared to my stodgy old professors in criminal justice." She pointed at Ray and snickered.

22

Elkins woke with a start. His pajamas were soaked with perspiration, and he felt tense and anxious. He looked over at the clock. It was just after 3:00 A.M. He got up, switched on the air conditioning, and went back to bed. Unable to sleep, he tried to organize all the facts in the Bensen case. He worked through the events two or three times. Eventually, he turned on a reading light and penned a list.

After turning off the light, he thought about the facts of the Hendrickson case. He organized and reorganized the data. He could do this better in the dark, clustering the different elements on a vaporous video, moving them around until he was satisfied with the pattern. Switching on the light again, he sketched the second pattern and then returned to darkness. He thought about Stephanie; he thought about Chesterton; he thought about Ellen. Yes, he would like to meet someone. He was attracted to Stephanie, but that would be too painful. He didn't want a relationship like that.

When he awakened next, it was with a sense of urgency. He had overslept. It was long past 7:00. He started the coffee, took a quick shower, retrieved the paper, and popped two pieces of whole wheat bread into the toaster.

He carried the paper out to the deck and made a second trip with a tray containing the pot of coffee, a cup, the toast and a container of margarine. He sorted through the paper, first scanning the national, then the international news.

Ray had moved to the sports section, perusing a long article on the NCAA's investigation of Division I football programs when the

Chesterton's terrier came crashing through the paper onto his lap. As he scratched the dog's ears, Banquo rolled his head nonchalantly toward the table and picked the remaining piece of toast off the plate. He hopped off Ray's lap and carried his prize to the edge of the patio, tore it in smaller pieces, wolfed down the chunks, wandered off to the edge of the deck, and looked back over his shoulder at Ray before scampering off to sniff under the deck.

Ray was almost through the article when the phone rang. It was Char Pascoe.

"Elkins, you'd better get over here. I'm at University Gardens. We have an apparent suicide. Are you ready for this?" She didn't wait for a response. "The woman, Constance Dalton, is a member of the English department, and there is a suicide note."

"Who found her?"

"A friend, they had planned to go to breakfast. When Dalton didn't answer her door, her friend opened the garage to see if the back door was unlocked. She found Dalton behind the wheel, motor still running."

"Get whatever help you need, get full photos, and have the place sealed off. Don't move the body until I look things over. Where are you in University Gardens?"

"It's the last unit on the left on Stadium Court."

"I'll be over in about twenty minutes."

"She's not going anywhere."

"Char, have you thought about becoming a pathologist?"

"Pathologist, no. Why?"

"You're getting that kind of a sense of humor."

He switched off the phone and returned to complete the article. He stacked the sections of the paper and carried them into the kitchen.

Banquo watched Elkins go into the house. The terrier climbed back onto the porch and inspected the area around Elkins's chair. Then he jumped up and walked around on the table. There were no additional scraps of toast to be had.

~~~~

23

By the time Elkins arrived, three police cars, an EMS unit, and an ambulance were parked at the end of Stadium Court. Two police cadets defended the yellow plastic ribbon from a cluster of onlookers, mostly adolescent boys sitting on their bikes and swapping lies in the warm, humid morning. Elkins paused, looked at the boys, and thought about when he was that age camping with friends, Jim and Butch, on an inland lake up in Michigan. That special memory vanished as he ducked under the plastic tape and walked toward the garage.

He paused for a few seconds and made a mental snapshot of the scene. The garage door was open. A late model Chrysler, steel blue, was in the center of a space big enough for two cars. The back wall of the garage near the house was covered with drywall, taped and painted; the side-walls were uncovered, studs and wiring exposed. On the right side of the garage a bicycle— black, dusty, English style, with a weathered wicker basket and flat tires—leaned against the wall. Behind it, a golf bag slouched into the corner. At the opposite corner of the garage was a door that he assumed opened into the townhouse. A plastic garbage can on wheels stood near the door.

The car door was also open. Char Pascoe, head and shoulders drooping forward as she explained something to an evidence technician, looked up and saw Ray approaching. When he reached her side, she said. "Dan's taken the usual series. I made sure he was extra thorough. Tell him if there is anything else that you want."

Elkins looked in at the body slumped against the gray leather up-holstery. He stood for a long moment taking in the scene, suddenly realizing that he was holding his breath. He turned and walked out into the sunshine with Pascoe following him. "I trust your judgment," he said, meeting her eyes.

"I just talked with Dr. Gutiérrez. She's coming over to examine the body," said Pascoe. "I knew you'd want to get a fairly accurate time of death."

"And the suicide note?"

"It's next to the body. Didn't you see it?"

Elkins shook his head rather sheepishly.

"I read it leaning over from the back seat. I wanted to get the scene photographed before I moved anything."

"What does it say?"

"Let me get it."

Pascoe went back into the garage. Ray waited, looking away from the townhouse at the fields of ripening corn turning gold under the hot morning sun.

Pascoe returned in a few minutes carrying an 8 1/2 by 11 sheet of paper in a clear plastic bag. She handed it to Elkins. He read the short note.

> *O me! what eyes hath Love put in my head,*
> *Which have no correspondence with true sight;*
> *Or, if they have, where is my judgment fled,*
> *That censures falsely what they see aright?*
> *If that be fair whereon my false eyes dote,*
> *What means the world to say it is not so?*
> *If it be not, then love doth well denote*
> *Love's eye is not so true as all men's: no,*
> *How can it? O! how can Love's eye be true,*
> *That is so vexed with watching and with tears?*
> *No marvel then, though I mistake my view;*
> *The sun itself sees not, till heaven clears.*
> *O cunning Love! with tears thou keep'st me blind,*
> *Lest eyes well-seeing thy foul faults should find.*

"What does it mean?" asked Pascoe.

"It's a sonnet, probably Shakespeare."

"I'm impressed. How did you know that?"

"I had an intro to Shakespeare when I was a sophomore or junior, the instructor did her dissertation on something to do with the sonnets. We spent most of the semester on the sonnets, hardly got around to the plays." Ray paused for a minute and carefully perused the text. "What does it mean? Just read it a couple of times, and you'll have it. The person who found the body, where is she?"

"The medical center. She was close to hysterical when I talked to her. I had Sergeant Jackson take her over. He's instructed to stay with her until he hears from me."

"Has anyone been in the house?"

"Just that friend, name's Mary Caswell. She's a librarian in the graduate library. She told me that after she discovered the body, she went in to use the phone. She said she knew from television that she shouldn't touch anything, so she came out right after making the call. And Jackson told me Caswell was in her car waiting when he got here."

Elkins looked west, his eyes moving along the horizon as if he was expecting to find something. Finally he said, "Right from the beginning this didn't feel right. Three deaths, all women, all in the English department. This is statistically improbable." He paused again, not pulling his focus from the distant horizon. "You know the dance, dust the house and car. See whose prints are there besides Dalton's and Caswell's. Look for anything suspicious. We need to check her voicemail, e-mail, talk to neighbors, friends, colleagues. And when that's completed, it's essential that we do that for the other two. I want to know everything and anything we can find out about these three women and what connections existed between them."

Pascoe nodded her agreement, "Our focus has changed."

"Yes," he answered. "Let's do a quick walk through, then I want you to process the place."

Elkins followed Pascoe through the door from the garage into the kitchen of the condo. The room was devoid of color—walls, floor, and appliances all in white—and with the exception of an empty bottle of Stolichnaya and a tumbler standing in the sink, all the surface areas in the kitchen—countertops and a small dining table—

were empty, not an envelope or a spoon or the hint of crumbs or any normal activity.

"After you dust the bottle and glass, I want you to check the contents of the trap," said Ray. "I want to know if someone poured vodka down the sink." He pointed toward the bottle. "Is that just a prop, part of the set, something designed to pull us away from the real facts of this death?"Look at this place," he said. "It's like she's never really moved in. There's nothing personal here. No art, no photographs, magazines, knickknacks. Nothing."

"It's a bit oppressive," Pascoe agreed. "Motel rooms have more personality." She stopped and looked at Ray. "You appear to be in a panic to get out of here."

He thought about her comment, and then responded, "I'm upset. Things are totally out of control. These people are dying, and we're clueless as to why." Their eyes met. "I'll run over to the medical center and see if I can learn anything from this Caswell woman."

Sergeant Jackson was waiting for Elkins near the admitting desk in the emergency room.

"How's the patient?" asked Ray.

"She was having difficulty breathing. They've admitted her. She's been sedated, but I think you can still talk to her."

Jackson led Elkins through the corridors, crowded with visitors, to a second story ward in the new south wing. They stepped off the elevator and walked to the nursing station. Elkins introduced himself to the nurse behind the counter and asked if he could have a brief conversation with Mary Caswell.

"You mean 27B," came the response from the nurse, fiftyish, with a wide jaw, a pronounced under bite, and several additional chins that gave her a bulldog appearance.

Elkins rephrased the request. "If 27B is Mary Caswell, would it be possible to ask her a few questions?"

"Do you have some identification?" she pressed.

Elkins had no police identification. He hadn't needed anything but his university ID and had never bothered to ask for any. With great pomp he pulled out his wallet and flashed a faculty library card with his picture in one corner. She nodded without focusing on it. The nurse came around from behind the desk. "She's just been given a strong sedative and may be asleep. You can only stay a few minutes. The patient has a history of heart trouble and has really worked herself into a state."

"We'll be brief, I promise," offered Elkins.

She held the door for them and then stood by the bed, her manner, menacing, to make sure they didn't upset the patient. She leaned over the bed and said, "Ms. Caswell, these two police officers want to ask you a few questions. I've told them they can only stay a few minutes."

The woman in the bed gazed at them glassy-eyed. She seemed to have difficulty pulling them into focus.

"Ms. Caswell, I'm Ray Elkins with the university police. Sorry we have to bother you at this time, We're trying to complete our investigation. Would you tell me what happened this morning?"

Caswell continued to gaze at them. After a long moment, in a halting fashion she started. "I went to pick her up. I was a few minutes early. There was no answer at the door. I tried the bell first, and then I knocked several times. I tried the door; it was locked. I became concerned. Constance is absolutely reliable. I just knew something was wrong, so I opened the garage door—we used to joke that we had the same code: 1-2-3-4. I was going to see if the door from the garage into the kitchen was open. When the door opened I could hear her car running. I looked in." She stopped. Elkins leaned forward. "The door was unlocked, so I went into the house, and I dialed 911. Then I went back outside to wait. That's all I know."

She looked at Elkins like she was trying to pull him into focus, then she drifted away. Her eyes closed.

The nurse exhaled heavily to indicate the interview was over. "She needs to sleep now, gentlemen. I'm sure she'll be in much better shape in the morning."

She herded them out of the room.

24

Elkins parked in his driveway and cut across the yard to the Chestertons' house. Stephanie, in denim shorts and a T-shirt, was on her hands and knees planting mums in a flower bed on the perimeter of their back deck. So as not to startle her, Elkins cleared his throat as he passed near her.

She looked up. "I was wondering when we would see you. We heard a couple of hours ago. Isn't it awful?"

"Where's Chesterton?" Elkins asked not responding to her question.

"He's in his study. Go on in. I think he's expecting you."

Elkins mounted the stairs, crossed the deck, and opened one of the French doors at the back of the kitchen. The house was cool and dark. He took off his sunglasses, slid them in his shirt pocket, and walked through the house to the study. The double doors were open and Chesterton was at his desk, books piled on either side, writing on a sheet of lined paper with a large fountain pen. He looked up as Elkins entered the room and rose, extending a hand across the massive desk.

"I thought you might be by to pick me up."

"Didn't want to put you through that again, Clifford."

"No problem, Ray. In fact, as strange as it sounds, these trips to the morgue have brought back some important memories."

"How's that?"

"When I was a lad I would often accompany my father to the hospital on weekends and school holidays. Those were the only times I really had him alone. He was too busy with his work and his teaching for us to do the usual kinds of excursions that boys and their fathers do. He would let me watch as he did an autopsy, explaining as he went. He was a born teacher and a good scientist."

"Did you ever consider medicine?"

"I arrived in New Haven convinced that I would go in that direction, but by the end of my freshman year I knew that wasn't my destiny. So much for family history, I expect you want me to tell you all I know about Constance Dalton."

Elkins nodded in the affirmative. Chesterton offered him one of two large, overstuffed leather chairs positioned on each side of a floor-to-ceiling gothic window.

"Can I offer you a drink?" Chesterton asked as he opened the doors on a large walnut bar.

"I would love one, but I have to take a pass."

"Yes, I understand. Duty and all that," responded Chesterton as he poured cognac from an etched glass decanter into a snifter. He planted himself in the chair across from Elkins.

"We have over sixty full-time members in the department, about half of them are not tenured," he began. "In addition, we have at least that many adjuncts and several dozen TAs. There are a lot of faculty members I don't really know. I mean, I know them by sight, and I know their specialty, but I don't know them. I've never spent any time with them. Never sat and chatted over a drink or a cup of coffee. Constance Dalton was someone I didn't know personally."

"Tell me as much as you do know."

Chesterton swirled the cognac. After a few moments he looked up at Ray and said, "She is, rather, she was starting her sixth year. Her specialty was medieval literature." He stopped and looked across at Elkins aware of the connections that Elkins was making. "Yes, medieval literature, just like Bensen and Hendrickson. I never would have thought that was a particularly hazardous occupation."

"How many medievalists are there?"

"We had five. Miller, that's Oscar Miller, he's close to retirement. I think he's spent his entire career here. Not a very pleasant fellow, looks a bit like a weasel, has a personality to match. Then we hired Bensen, followed by Hendrickson and Dalton. Finally, we have Jane

Arden. It was all so incredibly silly. I think I've already explained this to you."

"Yes?"

"Keith Beckner and his grand scheme to make this department an international center for graduate study in Medieval and Renaissance English literature in the American heartland. And as I mentioned, Keith moved up the administrative ladder, the graduate students never came, and we entered a period of rapidly declining enrollments in the humanities. Beckner's plan has turned out to be a total disaster for everyone involved."

"So what do these people teach?"

"Mostly intro to lit courses and freshman comp. Once a year they may be able to teach a survey course in English lit. Miller has an Old English course and the graduate seminar. The rest are not happy that they can't teach their specialty, and with the dreadful job market in English they don't have the opportunity to go anywhere else. They all know that their chances for tenure here are very limited. The same thing is true of the Renaissance lit people. Fortunately, none of them are dying."

"Dalton, would you tell me everything you know about her, what she looked like, her personality, friends, whatever?"

"You saw her?"

"I saw her body in the car, but I didn't get a good sense of her physically."

"She was very petite, almost frail, plain, but not unattractive. She seemed to be well liked, both by students and her colleagues. I know she was quite professional. And she was getting a lot of publication in her specialty.

"She came here with a husband. He was in physics or chemistry, one of the sciences. He got a tenure-track position in California several years back."

"Children?"

"That's what I was trying to remember. They had a son. I think when they separated the lad decided he wanted to live with his dad. There were rumors."

"Like?"

"I'm not quite sure. I try not to listen. I think the gist of things had to do with appearances. When people separate, the children usually stay with the mother."

"Any talk of another love interest?" Elkins asked.

"I don't know. I try to administer by focusing on professional issues, and I make a studied effort to stay as far away from the rumor mill as possible. English departments are just filled with whispers, backbiting, slurs, and insults. You know the old saw that's attributed to Wallace Sayre, 'Academic politics is the most vicious and bitter form of politics, because the stakes are so low.'" He paused, a smile spreading across his face. "I wish I could tell you more, but that's about all I know."

"How about Hendrickson?"

"There's a study in contrasts. Where Dalton was demure and not overly effusive, Hendrickson was loud, aggressive, yes, even obnoxious, but she was charming in her own way. She was bright, bawdy, humorous, a bit of a drunk, and, to use my mother's rather Victorian phrase, 'a wanton woman.'"

"Meaning?"

"Well," said Chesterton with a broad smile, "she was not restrained sexually."

"Could you be more specific?"

"Hendrickson was very open about liking sex and had numerous lovers, both male and female. If she were important or famous and rich, we'd be talking about her sexual addiction. She'd have gone off to one of those expensive clinics for treatment."

"Might Hendrickson have been involved with Dalton?"

"Interesting thought, but I would rather doubt it. They were too different. But who knows, the old cliché about opposites attracting one another."

"Let me backtrack for a minute. You had five medievalists, and three are now dead. It looks like two suicides and a traffic accident. This is statistically improbable. Who would like these people dead?"

Chesterton finished his cognac and stood. "Sure I can't get you a drink?"

"No, later perhaps."

Chesterton replenished his and settled back into his chair. He rolled the stem of the glass between his thumb and forefinger. "I think I know what you're fishing for. Not that I'm a specialist in genre fiction, but I've read enough of the crime stuff to know that motive is always the big thing. So, you're asking if these deaths were murder rather than what they appear to be, what would be the motive, or perhaps who would have a motive?"

"Exactly."

"Well, I've seen people try to do one another in over tenure, but in this case I don't think it works. Until Oscar dies or retires, none of these people had much hope of tenure. They all had a reason to bump him off. Pity they didn't. He's a wretched teacher and a loathsome human being."Before continuing, Chesterton swirled the dark golden liquid in the crystal globe and took an immoderate sip. "If they were doing in their rivals, they wouldn't be up to the blood and gore. It is much more polite to use rumor and innuendo." Chesterton gestured with his left hand, "You know, 'So and so's book on *Piers Plowman* was published by a third-rate university press and got lousy reviews.' These people get obsessed with things that no one beyond our cloistered walls has ever heard of, much less give a damn about."

"Sheila," Chesterton continued, "had her enemies, especially among the right-to-life people and the radical right. She was obstreperous and often mean-spirited, but within the department I don't think anyone hated her enough to want her dead. She was more of an embarrassment than anything else—the crazy aunt that you'd like to lock away in the closet when company comes. The people in the department just wanted her to go away. The other two were competent teachers and pleasant enough. I don't know everything that goes on, but I can't imagine they had any real enemies."

"How about students? Any disgruntled students who might have it in for one or more of these women?" asked Elkins.

"There's always that possibility. We have our share of nutcases on campus. In my early years in this profession I never heard of students making threats to faculty members, now it happens several times every term, especially near finals. And more and more, these are the problems that absorb my energy. Days can disappear by the time I talk to the faculty member, the student, your office, then involve the dean's office. And it's always boys, never women. It's the lads who are about to fail because they haven't done the work. These threats usually get them kicked out of the university, but I always live in fear that one of them is going to come back with a gun. It happens, Ray, you know it happens. I don't understand those lunatic politicians who think students should be able to carry concealed weapons on campus.

"Did any of these women receive threats from students?" asked Ray.

"Bensen was the only one students complained about. I have a complete record of those complaints in her personnel file. Students were upset because she would often not show up for class, and when she did, she wasn't prepared, and she seldom returned papers. Our students are getting to be better consumers. They are paying a lot for tuition, and when they're not getting their money's worth, they let me know."

"Any student complaints against the other two women?"

"This year Hendrickson was involved with a graduate student. That got a bit sticky. She chaired the young man's dissertation committee, but the other committee members rejected his work the first time through. Her colleagues were concerned that her judgment was influenced by her relationship with the student. When I confronted her, she asked why she wasn't allowed the same prerogatives as her male colleagues."

"How am I to interpret that?"

"I think there's only one way, Ray. She was a piece of work. Unfortunately, there was some truth to what she said."

"How about Dalton, any complaints or threats?"

"None. She was a smart, competent woman, a real professional. That said, Constance might have been very fragile emotionally, but I didn't know about that part of her life."

"This was sitting next to Dalton," said Ray. "It's a suicide note of sorts." He removed the plastic encased sheet from a folder and handed it to Chesterton.

Chesterton skimmed the verse. "You know what this is?"

"My guess is one of Shakespeare's sonnets."

Yes, very good. I'm not sure which, but it's one of the later ones."

He got up and walked to one of the floor to ceiling bookcases that surrounded the study. He studied a section of one shelf and finally removed a volume, opened it, and thumbed through it for a few moments. "Yes, 'Sonnet 148.'"

"What do you think?"

"Are you asking for an interpretation of the text giving consideration to the context in which it was found?"

"Yes."

"Well, I'm sure you've read it, and the meaning is quite clear. This is one of the later sonnets written to the mysterious Dark Lady. The poet was completely in love, or at least totally in lust for that woman. And she was, obviously not there for him. I think of Theseus's lines in *Dream*:

> *Lovers and madmen have such seething brains,*
> *Such shaping fantasies, that apprehend*
> *More than cool reason ever comprehends.*

"Or perhaps more simply put in the words of that old song, 'Falling in love with love is falling for make believe.' That said, this sonnet is a rather curious suicide note. It has always seemed to me that the kind of passion reflected in these sonnets is that of a young man, more about hormones then cognition. I would have thought Dalton was beyond that."He paused for a long moment and looked over at Ray,

"I'm just pulling at straws. I hope I'm not babbling on too much. Let me think. I'm not sure who was close to Dalton. Ask Alice Widdowson, my secretary, she's a bit of a snoop. I think she is on top of most of the department's gossip. I don't know what else to tell you." Chesterton finished his cognac and walked out with Ray. They paused on the back deck.

"Have any of my babblings helped?" Chesterton asked.

"Yes. I'm collecting pieces and trying to put them together in a way that will help me understand this chain of events."

Stephanie was still planting mums. She stood as Ray approached. "You okay?" she asked.

"I'll be better when I have some answers," he responded, giving her a weak smile.

25

Shortly after 9:00 on Friday morning, Ray Elkins parked in the staff parking lot near the rear entrance of the medical center and made his way toward the pathology department. Almost two weeks had passed since the death of Sheila Bensen, and now two of her colleagues were also dead.

"We're going to have to stop meeting like this," Dr. Kristin Gutiérrez affected a stern tone in her voice. "And you're late. Your assistant has already been here."

"So what does my assistant know that I don't?"

"Time of death. You know how exact I can be on that. Probably between 5:00 and 8:00 A.M. If you're into averages, 6:30 A.M. is a good number. Cause of death is carbon monoxide poisoning. Anticipating your question as to whether or not the deceased might have been placed in the car, I went over the body very thoroughly. There are no contusions, no tissue under the nails, nothing that would suggest a struggle."

"How about toxicology?"

"This is what I have so far, fairly high level of alcohol, I won't have the rest of the toxicology for several weeks. I didn't find any pills in her stomach. You know what I think?"

"Go ahead."

"This one appears to be a suicide."

Elkins looked thoughtful. "What else?"

"She didn't have anything that would kill her in the near future. She did have a small benign growth on the right ovary. I don't imagine it had been detected. It wouldn't have caused her any discomfort. Her tubes were tied, not recently. Her period was about to start in a day or two, and she had had an appendectomy, years ago. She also had diverticulitis. Other than that, she appeared to be in fairly good health, although her muscle tone was pretty flabby. She wasn't an athlete. In sum, the woman had no real health problems for someone in her early forties. That said, who knows what was going on in her head. That's where the real data is in these cases. Someday we might have a way of tapping into that, our own little flight recorders."

"I certainly hope not," said Ray.

"Yes, that would be horrible. Someone rambling through your thoughts."

"Is there any relationship between menstrual cycle and suicide rate?"

"I don't know that, I wouldn't be surprised. However, most of us aren't crazy when we're having our periods." She gave Ray a long look. "I'm not accusing you of buying into that lore, Elkins. However, the combination of alcohol, hormonal influences, and her emotional state might all contribute to her...."

"Actions."

"Yes, and if there is a history of depression, it could be a contributing factor. That's essentially what I meant." Her sudden change in expression indicated that the serious conversation was over. "Thanks for bringing me a body that's in good shape. The work's more enjoyable when the stiff isn't mashed or fried."

Elkins shook his head back and forth. "What will you do to my parts when I pass?"

"Don't worry, Elkins. I'll be totally discreet. And after I examine the contents of your skull, I'll stitch your face back on real tight. You won't have any wrinkles. You'll look terrific in the box. Everyone will say, 'Old Elkins, he hasn't looked that good in years.'"

"Thanks. Something to look forward to."

26

After leaving Dr. Gutiérrez, Elkins walked through a tunnel from the main hospital to the new Professional Arts Building. The tunnel system was a major design feature of the new complex, allowing barrier-free pedestrian traffic under roads and parking lots from the main hospital complex to the adjacent buildings that were continuing to sprout up from former corn and soybean fields. The pedestrian subways provided year-round protection from the sometime harsh Midwestern weather, the fierce winds and arctic blasts of winter and the scorching heat of summer. They also potentially offered a safe refuge for thousands of patients and staff in the event of a tornado threatening the area.

Ray avoided the elevator and took the stairs to the third floor hoping to find Dr. Margrave in. As he approached his destination, he saw Margrave hurrying in his direction from the elevator. "Elkins, good morning."

"Do you have a few minutes?"

"Let me check my schedule." Margrave unlocked the outer office. Elkins followed him through to the consultation room. Margrave sat at his desk, turned on the terminal, and brought up his calendar. "You're in luck. My first patient has canceled. What can I help you with?" he asked as he came around and sat, motioning Elkins to the patient's chair.

"Constance Dalton, was she a patient of yours?"

"Yes, she has been for several years. What's this about?"

"You don't know?"

"Know?"

"She was found dead yesterday morning. It appears to be a suicide."

"Oh, God. No. We were up to the cottage getting in a few more vacation days. Didn't return until late last night. What happened?"

"Carbon monoxide. A friend found her sitting in her car, motor running, garage door closed." Elkins paused for a moment and let the information soak in. "Did you think that she was suicidal?"

"That's a really hard question."

"How so?"

"With most people who talk suicide, it's usually an attention seeking device or a cry for help."

"How about Dalton?"

"She never mentioned it, but she was extremely closed, very hard to work with."

"What can you tell me about her?"

"You know, Elkins, after you were here last time I sought out the medical school's ethicist, name is Barney Carrick, old fellow, looks a lot like Freud."

"And?" pressed Elkins.

"He didn't call me back yet. And you need the information…" his voice trailed off.

"When there is an unnatural death, we have to make a complete investigation of the circumstances surrounding the death. In this case we are trying to determine whether or not this was a suicide."

Margrave rubbed his chin as he thought things over. He got up, opened a file drawer and after a few moments of looking, withdrew a folder. As he sat down again he looked over his notes. After a long silence Margrave looked up and said, "She never discussed suicide as an option, but somehow her taking her own life is not totally surprising. Constance was a very bright, complicated, and confused woman." He thumbed again before continuing. "She was an only child, her parents were close to forty at the time of her birth. By her account, they were two very neurotic people who were constantly giving her mixed messages. As an adult she was never able to unload any of this baggage. Constance was always trying to conform to their standards, and, at the same time, rebel against them. The irony, of course, was that her parents had been dead for years." Margrave looked up at Ray. "That's one of the dumb things we often do to ourselves, try to meet our parents' expectations long after they are gone."

"What can you tell me about her personal life?"

Margrave flipped to the front of the folder. "She was married, let's see, for about a dozen years and divorced about two years ago. They had one child, a boy. I imagine he's ten or twelve by now. He lives with his father. She didn't want custody. I worked with Constance and her husband in couple therapy before the divorce. He seemed like a decent sort of fellow, he was in physics. She would give lip service to trying to save the marriage, but I could tell her heart wasn't really in it. Shortly before the final split, she got involved in a lesbian affair. I didn't know it at the time. She brought it up when I started seeing her in individual therapy."

"Did she tell you with whom she was involved?"

"I don't know. All she ever said was the woman was a colleague. Well, I guess there is a little more." He looked at his notes. "She said she finally understood that one could have a richer relationship with a woman than a man because women have so much more emotional depth."

"But she never named the person?"

"No."

"She didn't mention Bobby Jo Hendrickson or Sheila Bensen?"

"No. She didn't use names. 'Colleague' was the term she always used."

"How about Mary Caswell. Ever mention her?"

"No. Constance had a great many taboos. Using names was one. Sex was something else she couldn't talk about. Shortly after this affair started, the marriage was over. She was really," Margrave paused, "I'm searching for the right word. I don't think she was openly hostile toward men, but she certainly was uncomfortable with most men. I was always curious about her relationship with her father. Might there have been some sort of physical, or psychological, or sexual abuse?"

"And?"

"She skirted the issue. I don't know. Perhaps there was nothing there, or maybe she wasn't ready to confront the issue. As she talked about her parents, they seemed to be a unit and she was the outsider. They had been together for almost twenty years when she arrived. From her description, they never quite figured out how to deal with her."

"How about her relationship with her son?" asked Ray.

"She didn't seem to connect to him emotionally. I didn't see any real maternal feelings or that she was conflicted over giving her husband custody. In fact I had a sense that she was happy to have that part of her life over. I never made much progress with Constance. We wasted her money and my time."

"And you think that suicide was a possibility?"

"Absolutely. She was very brittle, very fragile. As long as she kept her guard up, she could continue to function, but if something happened that would put a chink in her psychic armor, I'd think she'd collapse."

"Would the death of a lover do that?"

"Death, betrayal, or just a crack in her carefully constructed defenses." Margrave sat still for a minute, and then gestured with his left hand, pointing two fingers at Ray. "I guess I'm really angry. I hate it when a patient commits suicide. I'm angry with myself for not finding a way to get to them, and I'm angry with them for being so completely stupid. Anything else?"

"If this is a suicide, could Bensen's have triggered a copy cat behavior?"

"There's a chance of that. With adolescents, a suicide in a high school is often quickly followed by several more. In some instances the later casualties were close to the first victim, but often they didn't even know the person. They just saw death as an escape from the awful pain many teenagers experience. But in this case, I don't know."

"If Dalton had a strong emotional attachment to Hendrickson, the woman who was killed in the accident last week, might that...?"

"Again, I don't see that as a primary motivating cause for her decision. She was very conflicted, lots of dissonance. If there had been a close relationship with one of the women, that death might have been the triggering event. You know, the straw that broke the camel's back." Margrave closed the folder and dropped it on the top of his desk with his left hand. He sat and looked at Ray, finally asking, "Is there anything else?

After a long pause, Elkins responded, "No, not now, but I'm sure there will be."

"You know where to find me," responded Margrave, rising from his chair and grasping Ray's hand. "One more thing."

"What's that?" asked Ray.

"Did you ever start keeping a journal? We talked about it."

"I bought a blank journal," said Ray.

"That's the first step. Now you need to get some words on the pages."

27

Elkins walked up the back steps in the Campus Police building from the parking lot. As he headed toward his office, he was stopped at the desk of Bonnie Ferguson, the department receptionist. "There's someone in your office, Elkins. The woman's name is Jane Arden, a member of the English Department. She was quite insistent that she had to talk to you. And here are your phone messages, everyone wants to talk to you today, including Pearson."

"My lucky day," he responded as he headed down the corridor. The woman looked up, a smile crossing her face, as he entered his office.

"Good morning, " he offered his hand. She stood and grasped his hand firmly.

"Jane Arden. Sorry to crash in on you this way, your secretary suggested I wait for you here. Stephanie Chesterton introduced us."

"Yes, of course," he responded. He remembered her very clearly, but he was trying to appear as nonchalant as possible, his tone formal and professional "How can I help you?"

"I played tennis with Stephanie early this morning. She suggested I talk to you. Actually, I feel sort of embarrassed about it."

Elkins studied her as she talked—petite, tan, fine features, deep blue eyes, and a warm, attractive smile.

"I'm frightened."

"Do you want to tell me about it?"

"Under normal conditions, I'd probably laugh it off, but...." Tears filled her eyes and she reached for her purse. Elkins pushed a box of tissue across the desk.

"Why don't you tell me what's bothering you," he pressed.

"Do you know about the University's program at the state penitentiary?"

"I know we have one, but I've never been involved with it."

"I have been working in the program for four years. It's helped fill out my load, and the students are often more interesting than our average undergraduates. I have taught a number of courses there: freshman composition, intro to fiction, and world lit. It's not uncommon to have students for more than one course. I had one student, Arlin Merchant, in two different classes. His last class with me was this past fall. Months later I started getting letters. They were addressed to me at the English department, and I never responded to them. At first they were chatty and interesting. Then the letters changed."

"Let me guess, they became romantic?"

"Romantic at first, but soon the romance vanished. They became purely sexual and quite obscene. I contacted Jim Zeigler, the administrator at the prison who coordinates the program. He said that Merchant has been paroled."

Elkins studied the envelope, no return address but the postmark, although smudged, was clearly visible. He removed the letter, two pages of lined paper torn from a stenographer's pad, covered with an almost illegible scrawl in heavy black ink. He read the letter, pausing to read the last paragraph a second time. *I am watching you. I'm all ways out there waiting. I'll do all those things.*

Ray looked at her and said, "I can understand your concern. Are you sure this was written by...."

"Arlin Merchant. Yes, same handwriting, same paper, just like he used for my class."

"I'll put someone on this and find out what options are available to us. This might take a day or two. Obviously, you're going to have to be very careful. Where do you live?"

"In the faculty apartments, University Gardens on Varsity Court. That's the end court in the back near the railroad tracks."

Ray visualized the location. "It's fairly isolated out there. Anyone you can stay with for a few days while I try to find out what we're dealing with here?"

"Stephanie has invited me, but I don't want to do that. I want to be in my own place; I don't want some crazy dictating how I have to live. There is something you could help me with. Do you have anyone who can tell me if the locks on the doors and windows are adequate? I called University Housing. They said as long as the locks are working, they won't do anything. But the locks seem to be awfully flimsy. I'd like some expert advice on how I can make the place more secure."

"Well, that's a hard one. We're not organized like a city police force with a crime prevention bureau or officer. Let me think," Elkins tapped his finger on his desk, an outward manifestation of an inward grinding. "If you're going to be home late this afternoon, I'll try to stop by and see what I can suggest."

"That would be wonderful. I'll make it a point to be home."

"But," said Elkins, "let me say again. I think you should really consider staying with someone else."

She nodded her head, and he could tell by her expression she had no intention of doing so.

Elkins held up the letter, "May I keep this? We'll probably need this as evidence."

"I'm glad to be rid of it." She stood. "So I'll see you when?"

"I'll try to make it before six. I'll call before."

They shook hands and Elkins watched her go. Then he picked up the phone and dialed an extension. Char Pascoe was in his office within a few minutes.

"Read this letter. It was sent to a member of the English faculty by a former student in the penitentiary degree program."

She unfolded the letter and read, and then looked up, "Has a way with words, but he's no Browning."

"Where did that come from?" asked Ray.

"Hey, you think you were the only one to take survey classes. I thought Browning was pretty hot."

"And Arlin is not," said Ray. "So follow up on this. The contact person at the prison is Jim Zeigler. Find out who Arlin Merchant's parole officer is, and the conditions of the parole. And find out what options we have in dealing with this. The woman is scared and rightfully so."

"This is the kind of assignment I like. I like to nail bastards like this."

"She complained about door locks. I said I would come by later this afternoon and take a look. Changing topic, what did you find in the Dalton apartment?"

"We dusted the house for prints and went over the place very thoroughly for other possible evidence. A copy of Shakespeare's sonnets was next to her computer. Her prints are on the keyboard, but we couldn't find a copy of the text saved on the hard drive. I did print a couple of lines and had them compared with the note we found in the car. The lab confirmed the note was printed on the same paper." She paused and looked at Ray for a long moment before continuing. "The house is sealed, just in case you want to have another look around. Dalton's ex-husband and son are flying in this evening. I've got a suite for them at the Union. He's making funeral arrangements. I've told him he won't have access to the house for several days."

"I'm always impressed by how thorough you are."

"Elkins," she said with a smile, "you like me because I'm so much like you, a compulsive, type-A, workaholic—the kinds of traits that drive most people crazy. Additionally, I'm better organized than you, and neater, too." She stood and started to leave the office, stopping briefly and turning toward him again. "If you were only ten years younger and rich, we'd have a great future."

28

While Elkins was on the phone, Reda Rudd settled into a chair in his office. She dropped her backpack in the next chair, opened it and extracted a folder. She removed a sheet from the folder and placed it in front of Elkins.

Elkins, obviously listening to the person at the other end of the phone, nodded to Reda. Then his eyes traveled down the article.

Faculty Suicide Stuns University

Professor Constance Dalton, 42, was found dead in her car in the closed garage of her townhouse Thursday morning. The motor was still running at the time the body was discovered. The cause of death has been officially listed as carbon monoxide poisoning. The body was discovered by a friend, Ms. Mary Caswell, a reference librarian in the graduate library.

Ms. Dalton, a specialist in medieval and Renaissance literature, was beginning her fifth year at the university. She was divorced and the mother of an eleven year old son. It is believed that the child resides with his father.

This is the third death of a member of the department of English in less than two weeks. Ms. Sheila Bensen died in a fall from the university carillon. That death, while still under investigation, is listed as a probable suicide. Five days later, Ms. Bobby Jo Hendrickson, died in a traffic accident.

Reda Rudd dropped a second clipping in front of Elkins. In ballpoint at the top it was marked, "Editorial, *State Journal.*"

Faculty Deaths Teach Important Lesson.
The members of the Legislature had better sit up and take notice of what is happening at State. The recent deaths of three faculty members is just another indication of the type of individuals being recruited to educate our sons and daughters.

In less than two weeks there have been two suicides, and a bourbon soddened professor lost her life in a fiery late-night traffic accident. These are just the most recent examples of what's been going on at State for years.

It's time that the members of the Legislature got the message that the people of this state are getting tired of having their hard earned dollars taxed away to support a bunch of drunks, psychotics, drug users, feminists, and sodomites.

Even worse, we're getting tired of having lifestyles and values modeled for our youth that we find reprehensible. It's time the legislature sent a message to Chancellor Pearson that they're not going to tolerate this kind of behavior anymore. It's time to pull the purse strings tight and get some reform started.

"Yes, I've just read it," Elkins said into the receiver. He looked across at Reda and shook his head from side to side. His tone changed, and showing obvious anger he retorted, "And I want to remind you, sir, that I've kept you informed every step of the way. We're not creating these events. We're on the receiving end. We are investigating each one thoroughly. No one will be able to criticize the quality of the police work." There was a pause as he listened to the other party. Then he responded, "If there are any new developments, I'll get back to you immediately." He tossed the receiver at the cradle.

"Let me guess," Reda said with a mocking smile. "Pearson?"

"You've got it. You brought the editorial in just at the right moment. I was able to see what set him off. Pearson doesn't do well with criticism, especially if it's in the *State Journal*. He's convinced that the members of the legislature get most of their information from that rag and, unfortunately, he's probably right."

"How can he take those assholes seriously? Most members of the legislature are unemployable in any other kind of work."

"He has to. They determine our budget. And the *State Journal,* their editorial policy, as provincial as it is, is probably pretty close to what most of their readers believe. Probably quite close to what Pearson believes, too."

"Depressing thought," she responded.

"It's a reality."

"I know it is, but one I choose not to believe. It's too painful." Rudd pointed to the first article. "I talked to Pascoe about the Dalton death. My article is based on that. Is there anything new?"

"No, you know what I know."

"Isn't this too much of a coincidence?" she asked.

"Yes. Too much, but I don't have any other explanation. Unlikely, chance, rare, statistically improbable, you can generate all kinds of adjectives, but we still don't have the smallest bit of evidence of foul play in any of these deaths. Have you heard any interesting rumors?"

"Yes. The NCAA is out to get our football program. The major brewers are in collusion to force up the price of kegs this fall—things like that. The death of a few English department members of the doesn't generate much interest in the undergraduate world."

The phone rang again. Elkins said, "Let me take this call." As he started to talk, Reda gathered up her backpack. She waved on her way out.

29

Ray asked Pascoe to accompany him on the short trip to Dalton's townhouse in University Gardens. During the ten minute trip Pascoe gave him a summary of Arlin Merchant's criminal history. "He entered the juvenile justice system at thirteen. He was in and out of Branch County's juvenile center, more in than out, until he was sixteen. Then he prepped at Pine Lake Center for Juvenile Offenders. When he left at eighteen, he had managed to earn a GED. By the time he was twenty he was a guest of the state again, only this time with the big boys."

"What for?"

"He had gone into the auto parts business. He would steal cars and strip them. From the air a state police pilot looking for marijuana plots noticed a wood lot on a farm filled with cars. They sent someone to investigate and found twenty-some late model cars, partially stripped. The woods were located on Merchant's grandfather's farm. I talked with the sheriff in Branch County. He said the grandfather had lost it, probably didn't notice what the kid was doing."

"Any other convictions?"

"No, that's it."

"Where is he now?"

"He's back in Branch County, and get this, the parole board helped get him a job washing trucks and doing light maintenance for the county road commission. His parole officer wasn't available. He's supposed to call me tomorrow. I'm also meeting with an assistant prosecutor tomorrow to see what our options are."

"You did all that in a couple of hours," Ray formed his question as a statement, but Pascoe understood that he was complementing her.

She was embarrassed and changed the subject by pointing to the weedy and wilted flower beds in front of the townhouse complex and asking, "Is that why they call this University Gardens?"

"God, you're becoming a cynic," retorted Ray. "I understand that the horticulture department once occupied this area. They had a classroom building, greenhouses, and gardens. When the university quadrupled in size in the sixties and early seventies, the College of Agriculture—including the horticulture department—got a beautiful new facility on West Campus. At that time there was a severe housing shortage, both for students and faculty. The university built all those high-rise dorms, and this one complex of condos for faculty members."

The police line was still in evidence and a patrol car was parked in the drive, the front of the car facing the street. As they approached, a young woman in the department's light blue summer uniform with the white lettered 'Cadet' patch at her shoulder emerged from the car.

"Boring assignment?" asked Ray, as the young woman unlocked the door for them.

"This morning I got to meet all the neighborhood boys on their way to school. Since then it has been very quiet."

After they were in Dalton's townhouse, Pascoe asked, "What's our purpose here?"

"Two things, and then I just want to have a look around."

"What specifically?"

"I want to see if she has any other liquor, and I want to look for medications." Ray went into the kitchen. "You dusted the cabinet doors?"

"We dusted everything."

"Any alcohol?"

"There were a few bottles in one of the cupboards. I think they were in here." She opened a cupboard next to the sink. "Yes, this is the one."

Ray pulled on some rubber gloves, dropped to one knee, and looked in. "Let's see, four bottles. Two Jack Daniel's, one close to empty and one unopened. And two bottles of gin, one half gone and the other unopened. I've always wondered how Queen Victoria would have felt about having her picture on a bottle of gin."

"Who?"

"That lovely lady," he said, holding the bottle so she could see the label. "Check these for prints, all four bottles." Elkins pulled the refrigerator door open. He noted the bottles of diet tonic water, one half empty, three more unopened, and the two unsliced limes. He let the refrigerator close.

"Oh, by the way, what did you find in the trap?" Ray asked.

"Nothing, just soapy water," Pascoe replied and followed him up to the second story. He checked around the nightstand, a two-shelf arrangement with a clock radio on the lower shelf and a reading light on the top.

"I thought I was organized," Pascoe observed as they looked around. "Everything here is just perfect."

"But perhaps not perfect enough," said Ray. His irony wasn't lost on her.

He went into the bathroom. It was papered in a pastel flower design, and curtained with a material that picked up the colors in the paper, or vice versa. The bath and hand towels were carefully hung, they looked to Ray like they had never been used. Something about the room repelled him. It looked as though every attempt had been made to disguise the room's primary function.

Elkins opened the medicine chest—toothpaste and floss on the first shelf, makeup, other toiletries on the second shelf, and medications on the top shelf. Everything was neatly arranged alphabetically, all the labels facing the front. He looked at the bottles: aspirin, Tylenol, and two bottles with prescription medications. He could read the label on the first, an antibiotic, the prescription two years out of date. He turned the second bottle. *Bobby Jo Hendrickson* was typed in following *Patient's Name,* and *Seconal 100 mg* was typed at the bottom of the label. He pointed to the bottle. "You'll be interested in this. Check it for prints and find out why this guy was prescribing this for Hendrickson. Then we'll have to try to figure out how Dalton ended up with it."

Pascoe, with gloved hands, picked up the bottle and dropped it into a plastic evidence bag. "Anything else in here you want?"

"No, that's all. I'm finished for now, but let's keep the place secure for a few days, just in case we want to do a bit more work here."

30

It was after 8:00 P.M. when Ray completed the day's paperwork, a task that he hadn't been able to start until after 5:00. As he arranged the folders on his desk, he remembered his promise to check the door locks at Jane Arden's townhouse and kicked himself for not doing it earlier when he and Pascoe were in the area.

He found her number in the on-line staff directory and called, apologizing for not getting over to her place earlier in the day. Arden inquired whether he had eaten. When he said he hadn't, she invited him to come over for dinner, adding that she would feel better if she had his advice on the locks, that she wanted to make her place as secure as possible. Ray looked back at the screen to check the address and said that he would be by in about a half an hour. He put the paperwork on his secretary's desk and had a brief conversation with the evening shift commander. Pascoe had scheduled increased patrols in University Gardens, and Ray wanted to confirm that that request had been implemented.

When he walked back to his office to pick up his jacket, Ray looked at the two boxes Pascoe had dropped off before she left for the day. One contained a new Glock 19 pistol, the other a shoulder holster. Since becoming the acting director of the campus police, Ray had put a uniform weapons policy in place. Under the department's former leadership, officers had been required to provide their own side arms. Unfortunately, there had been a tendency on the part of a few of the department's "cowboys" to opt for "Dirty Harry" sized weapons. Ray wanted to get rid of the Hollywood props as he worked to develop a competent and professional police unit.

Ray lifted the pistol, first checking the safety. He hadn't owned or even handled a pistol or any other kind of weapon for years. He put the Glock back in the box, then thought of his directive that campus police officers should carry their weapons at all times. *This too shall pass,* he thought as he pulled on the shoulder holster. He looked forward to the time in the near future when he would be relieved of this administrative role and return to teaching.

Pascoe had spent fifteen or twenty minutes helping him adjust the fit of the holster, much of the time he stood with his arms lifted as she fiddled with the straps. Sliding the magazine in the base, he chambered a round, rechecked the safety, and secured the pistol in the holster. Ray pulled on his sport coat, and adjusted the position of the holster. He was bothered by the bulk of his new appendage, sure that its presence would be obvious to even the most casual observer.

By the time Ray got to University Gardens, the last remnants of a sunset had been obliterated by the heavy, black clouds of a storm rapidly approaching from the west. He could see lightening in the clouds, but the flashes were still too far away for the thunder to be heard.

The front door opened just as he was reaching for the bell. Arden unlocked the screen door and ushered him in. Ray noted that the floor plan of Arden's townhouse was the same as Dalton's, only reversed. There were four townhouses per unit; the two on the right hand side were oriented one way, the two on the left the other.

Ray looked around the living room. Although the interior space was the same, he was instantly struck by the contrast between Dalton's and Arden's decorating. Dalton's compulsiveness was reflected by cleanliness, order, and a chilling perfection.

Arden's decorating was warm, colorful, and inviting; the furniture was elegantly simple and tastefully arranged. Oriental rugs covered the hardwood floors, and the two oil paintings were appropriate in size to the wall space they occupied.

Arden was wearing a pastel pink linen dress, the color highlighting her tan and giving her, thought Ray, a softer appearance than she had in his office. She smelled of soap and shampoo.

"Should I start here with the front door?" he asked.

"Well, you can if you want to, but you can also sit down, and I'll get you a drink."

"Let me look at the doors and window, then I'll consider the drink."

Ray inspected the lock on the front door, then he checked the lock on the entrance from the garage. "Both locks should be replaced," he announced, "They are old and worn, and deadbolts should be added to each door. What kind of lock does your patio door have?"

"Just that little clip thingamabob on the handle. Most of the time that doesn't seem to catch." Arden led him to the patio door at the back of the kitchen. Ray played with the lock. It was damaged and could only be engaged with much jiggling. "This needs to be replaced," said Ray, "but even when it's working right, it doesn't provide much security. You can pop one of these locks with a screwdriver or a tire iron. If you get a length of board and jam it in here…," Elkins dropped to his knees and showed her where the board should be placed, "it's almost impossible to open the door."

"How about windows?" she asked.

Elkins looked at the window behind the sink, a sliding unit with an aluminum frame. "This would also be easy to force. You can get clamps at the hardware store that fasten to the tracks here, bottom and top. They're inexpensive and effective."

"Anything else I should do?"

"It's very important that you become especially vigilant and careful. Try to move about in daylight hours as much as possible so you can see if there is anyone around, and if so who it is. If you come home and there's a strange car parked in the area, or if you see a light you don't remember leaving on, anything unusual, don't go in. Call and we'll have officers accompany you and check out your home. I've increased patrols in this area, and they have specific instructions to keep an eye on your townhouse. Monday, I'll call maintenance to replace the locks, install deadbolts, and do something for that patio door. And I'll suggest that they need to check every lock in the entire complex and probably replace most or all of those as well."

"Lots of luck," Jane said with a smile. "As I told you this afternoon, the woman at university housing said that if the locks weren't broken...."

Elkins cut her off. "I've had a bit more experience working the bureaucracy. When you make something a safety issue, people tend to get excited and usually take action."

"I would appreciate that."

Elkins rested against the counter on the back wall. Jane was directly across from him leaning against the counter that separated the U-shaped kitchen alcove from the living room. As Ray looked at her, he could sense her discomfort.

"Yes?" he prompted, reading in her eyes that a lot was going on.

"Well, there's so much that's out of my control. I feel like I'm under house arrest. Without your help, I can't get locks fixed. You say I should be careful about moving around after dark." She paused, then continued, her voice and body language showing her frustration. "I'm very self-sufficient. I don't like this, I don't like this at all."

"It's not a good situation. I'm sorry that you have to put up with it. In a few days we'll have a better handle on this Merchant character and, hopefully, we'll have a clearer idea what our options are."

"I appreciate your efforts. I was feeling very vulnerable. Thank you. You must be starving." She didn't wait for a response. "Let me get you a drink. Stephanie says you drink Scotch."

"I'll take a pass on the drink now, thank you. Perhaps a glass of wine with dinner," he responded. Ray noticed the bottle on the counter, the brand he preferred. *Stephanie*, he thought. He became uncomfortable.

"I have some fresh pasta and pesto and the makings for a salad."

Elkins nodded. "Anything I can do?"

"How about shredding some Parmigiano?"

"I can do that."

"The cheese is in the fridge, the grater and bowl are there," she pointed.

Ray found the hunk of cheese, removed the butcher paper wrapping, and started putting hunks of cheese through the stainless steel mill, sampling a bit in the process.

"And when you finish that, there's a baguette in the oven that needs to be sliced. Put it in here," she said, sliding a cloth-lined wicker basket in his direction. The thunder and lightening were intensifying, and the wind suddenly picked up. Jane crossed the room and closed the patio door. The lights flickered, went out, and came on again a few seconds later.

"I think it's time for candles," Jane said, first lighting two candles in the kitchen area and then the candelabra on the dinner table. As they began to carry food to the table the lights went out again. This time they didn't come back on.

"Good timing on your part," said Ray.

"What can I tell you? In life, timing is everything," she quipped, giving Ray a warm smile. "Would you like a glass of Merlot," she asked showing him the label, "or would you prefer something else?"

"Merlot would be fine."

"And can I take your coat? I should have asked your sooner."

"I'm a little chilled at the moment. I would like to keep it on, thank you," Ray said, embarrassed that Jane would see him packing.She seated Ray at a table near the patio door, and she sat across from him. As he sipped the wine, Ray felt warmth beginning to flow through his body. He hadn't had anything to eat since late morning, a carton of yogurt consumed on the run.

After they began eating, Ray sensed that Jane was beginning to relax. The tension engendered by talk about security and the underlying reason for his visit seemed to vanish. They fell into an easy conversation.

Ray had found Jane attractive the first time they met. By candlelight she was even more so. She told him about her trip to England in June. Ray mentioned the article he had recently read on Cornwall in the travel section of the *Times*. Jane, with much animation, told him about an extended holiday she had had in Cornwall when she was doing post-doctoral work at the University of London. Elkins watched her and her shadows move. The shadows mimicked her movement, but were made even more spirited by the flickering of the candles. Outside the wind howled and cascading rain pounded on the roof and windows.Arden was in mid-sentence when the glass in the door wall exploded into the room, followed by a blast of cool, wet air. Ray pulled Jane to the floor, asking if she was unharmed, then dialing 911 on his cell phone. He slid through the shattered opening and moved along the side of the building, unholstering his pistol. Lightening flashed, and he saw someone sprinting along the thick hedge that defined the back perimeter of the complex, beyond which was a railroad embankment. As Ray pursued, he saw the figure disappear through the hedge, a dense, tall thicket designed to muffle the sounds of passing trains.

He pushed through the line of shrubs, stumbling as he came down the steep embankment. Lightening flashed again. He could see a dark form sprinting away from him, running in the low area between the two sets of tracks. Ray regained his footing and followed, crossing the first set of tracks, running between the parallel ribbons of steel. He could see the headlight of an approaching locomotive; the figure he was pursuing silhouetted by the brilliant beam. He could hear the locomotive's bell, the pounding of the huge diesels, and then the blast of the horn sounded almost continuously as the engineer tried to warn away the approaching runners.

The figure crossed over the second track and disappeared into darkness. Ray waited as two massive tandem locomotives lumbered by, the earth shaking, their roar filling his ears. Then he crossed over the second set of tracks and ducked for cover as he was suddenly caught in the beam from the receding engine. Ray felt his right foot become wedged, and then he tumbled violently forward.

31

Within minutes of Elkins' 911 call, a squad car arrived at Jane Arden's townhouse in University Gardens. The first officer on the scene, a June graduate of the criminal justice program, adrenalin coursing through his system as he responded for the first time ever to a shooting, secured the area and tried to calm Arden. Two more campus police officers, two sheriff deputies, and Charlene Pascoe followed moments later. Arden told them about creeping to the side of the patio door after Elkins rushed out. She explained how she watched Ray pursue the black-clad shooter across the lawn to the hedge, their trajectory illuminated by strobe-like flashes of lightening. Arden said she could hear the pounding of the passing locomotives and something that might have been a shot.

Pascoe led the way through the heavy rain with four other officers in her wake. Once beyond the hedge, the powerful beam from the locomotive lit the area as it crept back toward the scene. The engine ground to a halt as the officers moved across the track. Pascoe spotted Elkins as soon as she got to the center of the second set of tracks. He was face down in a pile of old railroad ties, chunks of concrete, and other debris below the railroad embankment. As she knelt at his side and felt for a carotid pulse, she could hear someone shouting for EMTs. Then she saw a nylon jacket dropped over his back.

When the EMTs were at her side, she moved out of their way. She retrieved Elkins' weapon, checking the safety, then zipping it into a jacket pocket. Charlene paused for a moment to gather herself, then climbed the next embankment. With the exception of automobile lights on distant roads, the terrain was cloaked in darkness. Then the lights started to flicker on, and she was able to gain her orientation. In the distance were the football stadium and basketball arena. Other buildings and facilities dotted the square mile area, connected by roads and paved parking lots. Acres of open land, used only on football Saturdays for parking, stretched from where she stood to the brightly lit buildings and lots. "If anyone had a car up here, they're long gone," one of the two officers who had joined her observed.

"I want this area closed off," she said. "No use rummaging through here in the dark, but tomorrow morning we need to see if the shooter left anything behind. Also, I want to see if we can recover any brass." The rain was still falling, no longer the heavy showers, now just a steady drizzle.

Pascoe moved back to the top of the embankment and watched as Elkins, now secured to a backboard, was carried up the opposite bank toward a waiting ambulance; she could see the unit's flashers just beyond the wall of shrubbery. Then she carefully negotiated her way down the slippery bank to talk to the railroad engineer, who had been watching the scene for several minutes from the tracks near the front of his idling locomotive. She was quickly able to determine that while the engineer was frantically trying to warn the runners away from his locomotives, he didn't see either man clearly. Pascoe wrote down his name and phone number and said that she would need to talk to him again.

When she returned to Arden's apartment, the campus police shift commander, a senior department member—had arrived and taken control of the scene. Jane Arden was just being loaded into a van to be taken to the medical center for attention to a cut on her hand. Charlene discussed with him the areas that needed to be protected until she could process them in the morning, and then she walked to her car and slid behind the steering wheel.

Charlene sat for several minutes in the quiet. She thought about the first time she met Professor Ray Elkins. She was a sophomore in college, nineteen, in a class with twenty men and three women taking the first course in the curriculum, Criminology and Criminal Justice. Early in the semester one of the men, a burly football player, made a crack about women in police work. Elkins stopped the discussion and said, "Gentlemen, in my time working as a police officer, I have never found anything that a man could do better than a woman."

"How about physical strength?" the guy asked. She remembered the smug look on his face.

"First, women can be trained to use their physical strength to their advantage. Given the appropriate training, a woman can be just as effective as a man. Second, women tend to use their intelligence, rather than relying on brute strength to get them through difficult situations. If extreme force is necessary, a ninety pound woman is just as deadly as a two hundred pound man."

She tried to hold back the tears and then let them flow. She knew Elkins wouldn't call that weakness; he'd call it strength. More than once she had seen his eyes mist over. He was a very sensitive man. That's what she remembered and admired so much. Charlene also thought about how he seemed different now than when she was first introduced to him more than a decade before, laconic, sometimes taciturn. She knew he was still struggling with a great loss in his life.

Her thoughts flipped back to her encounter with Elkins as a teacher. He was constantly challenging conventional wisdom, forcing his students to confront their beliefs, values, and prejudices. He was persistently pushing them to expand their understanding of the rest of humanity.

She remembered his favorite phrase. "The key to successful investigations is to be open to all the possibilities. If your understanding of humanity is limited, if you are controlled by prejudices and stereotypes, your ability to conduct intelligent investigations will be limited. The more you know, the greater the width of your vision, the more effective you're going to be."

Pascoe reflected on how pleased she had been earlier this spring when Elkins called trying to recruit here for a management job in a troubled department. She was flattered that he would think of her, given his many students over the years. And he had reached out to her at a time when she was starting to look for new challenges.

Pascoe turned the ignition key, took a few deep breaths, and headed for the medical center.

32

It had been a long night of waiting for Charlene Pascoe. Sometime after 2:00 A.M. one of the trauma physicians, a tall imposing woman, ebony skinned with a rich operatic voice, explained that Elkins had regained consciousness, but that he had apparently suffered a severe concussion and was in the process of getting a CT scan. Exhausted, Pascoe went to her apartment, but she had trouble falling asleep, the adrenalin from the evening's events still coursing through her system.

Before 9:00 A.M. she was back at the hospital, first checking on Ray's condition and then finding Jane Arden's room. Pascoe knocked on the jam of the open door before entering. Arden was sitting in bed, her left hand wrapped in a gauze bandage. An untouched breakfast tray with toast and anemic looking scrambled eggs rested on a stand across the bed.

Pascoe identified herself.

"Were you there last night?" asked Arden.

"Yes. You were quite shaken and had a nasty cut or two. I saw an EMT attending to you."

"It's all a blur. There were lots of people. I was so frightened."

"How is the hand?" asked Pascoe.

"Sore, now that local anesthesia has worn off. The surgeon said it was a long, deep gash, but he didn't find any damage to tendons or ligaments. Guess I was lucky. I don't even remember getting hurt. One of your people pointed out that I was bleeding."

"Are you up to answering some questions?"

"No problem. I don't even know why I'm still here," said Arden. "I need you to tell me everything that happened from the time Elkins got to your house until the time the police arrived on the scene." As she was saying this Pascoe was preparing to take a statement. She pulled a chair close, placed a small recorder on the bed, opened a steno pad to a clean page, and tested a ballpoint on the margin of the page, moving the pen in swirls until it produced a thick black line.

Pascoe began, "To the best of your memory, exactly what happened."

"Where do I start?"

"Start at the beginning. It's helpful if you can keep things in chronological order. I know that's not always easy to do."

Arden closed her eyes and rubbed her forehead. She opened them again and looked over at Pascoe. "It was about 9:00, perhaps a few minutes before. Elkins said he'd come over about 6:00 to check the locks; he called about 8:00 and said he was running late. I asked if he had eaten. He hadn't, so I invited him to have dinner." She paused briefly, then asked. "You know why he was checking the locks?"

"He showed me the letter, and I've done some research on Arlin Merchant." Pascoe waited for Arden to continue.

"It was getting dark about that time. It hadn't started to storm yet, but it was close. You could see the lightening on the horizon. Elkins inspected the locks on the windows and doors and told me what needed to be done. He offered to help get the university housing office to replace the locks. As I threw together a quick dinner, pasta and salad, the storm was intensifying. We sat down to eat and the lights went out. They came back on again, then went out a second time. I already had candles burning, and we started to eat. Then there was breaking glass. Elkins pushed me to the floor and told me to stay there. He made a call on his cell and went out the patio door. I was absolutely petrified. I wish he had stayed with me. I crawled over to the door and watched him run along the hedge at the back of the property. A minute or two later I heard the sirens. The first officer stayed with me. I could hear a lot of voices, but I didn't know what was happening. I remember the EMT coming, and then I think I saw you. That's about all I remember." She paused, and then asked, "Can you feel a bullet?"

"What do you mean?" asked Pascoe.

"I remember when the window exploded I felt something go by me, like wind. It was really close. I was wondering if that could have been the bullet?"

"I don't know. I think that's possible."

"My imagination is probably going wild." She paused, "I remember someone bandaging me up. They put me in an ambulance. After my hand was stitched someone gave me a hypo. I just woke up 30 minutes ago. So what happened, did you catch Merchant?"

"I will be talking to him today. We haven't established that he was involved."

"Elkins didn't catch the person?"

"No"

"Will he be coming by?"

Pascoe took a deep breath and considered her response. "Actually, he was injured last night. He's going to be okay, but he's going to be out of commission for a few days."

"What happened...?"

"It appears that he had a bad fall. He has a concussion."

"Oh, how awful." They sat in silence. "What happens now?"

"I need to ask you a few more questions. As I told you, I'll be talking to Merchant this morning. And he has clearly threatened you. What I need to know... are there other people who...you know... like old love interests, former spouses...people who might want to harm you?"

Arden absorbed the question and was slow in responding. "I was briefly married in graduate school. We've been divorced for years. He's got a new wife and two small children, lives in Vermont. There was never any hostility in our parting, just sadness. And I don't have any recent boyfriends lurking about. Nothing like that."

"And other than Merchant, you have received no threats?"

"None."

"You haven't seen or felt anything that's made you uncomfortable in recent weeks or months?"

"Me personally, no. That said, the deaths in the department have been shocking. I don't remember anything like that, never. But one was a suicide and the other a tragic accident. I don't know about Constance Dalton, I heard she had medical problems."

"How well did you know the three women?"

"They were colleagues. We'd see one another at meetings, I'd pass one or another in the halls or the department office occasionally."

"So you weren't close?"

"No. I didn't really know any of them well. We didn't do anything socially. But what does their deaths have to do with my situation?"

"Probably nothing, I'm just playing with possibilities." Pascoe closed her notebook and retrieved her recorder.

"My understanding is that you can be released later this morning. I don't want you to leave here until we find a safe place for you to stay for a few days."

"What's happening with my condo?"

"It's part of the crime scene. And then some repairs will be needed before you can return."

"I could probably stay with the Chestertons," Arden said.

"Let me think on that. I'll call you later this morning, and we'll get something in place."

"So before you go, tell me about Elkins again."

"He's being held for observation. I'm sure he'll be fine in a few days."

"So he goes way beyond what's expected, and he get's hurt."

"It could have been so much worse," said Pascoe. "It could have been so much worse," she repeated softly.

33

After visiting the medical center, Pascoe called the Sheriff of Branch County to request that Merchant be brought in for questioning. Then she drove over to University Gardens to work with the crime-scene team. They were already assembled and waiting for her, one regular member of the department, Bill Baker, and ten cadets—dressed in blue coveralls. Her greatest concern was to control the eagerness of the cadets so evidence wouldn't be overlooked or trampled.

Pascoe started the process by entering the condo and locating the bullet hole in the side of the island that separated the kitchen from the living room. She looked at the position of the chairs and the patio door and visualized the path of the bullet. She gathered the interns around her in the back yard and gave them specific instructions about how the search would be conducted. With Baker's assistance, she had the interns line up and separate themselves by fully extending their arms. "This is what I want you to do. We will move as a group slowly across the lawn until we get to the hedge. If you see anything unusual, call out and either Sergeant Baker or I will come to you. Don't touch anything. We need your eyes. Questions?"

"What are we looking for?" asked a tall, gangly kid whose long legs gave a high-water effect to his coveralls. "We're looking for anything that the shooter might have dropped that would help us ID him. When we get to the hedge and beyond we're especially looking for brass—shell casings."

"Maintain your distances and stay in line. We're going to move forward very slowly," instructed Sergeant Baker. The cadets carefully covered the expanse of lawn, stopping at the hedge. Pascoe had them move through the few openings in the thick brush. By the time they had lined up again, she was standing on the railroad embankment with a bullhorn in hand. "Let's close it up, guys. One arm's length between you. Be careful, it's steep. Let's go real slow." Other than plastic grocery bags, beer cans, and filters from degrading cigarette butts, nothing was found. She divided the teams and had them move down the tracks to the area where Elkins had been found. Then she brought the whole team to the left side of the tracks and they swept forward for a hundred yards, covering the area from the tracks to the top of the embankment. Eventually they moved along the outside of the embankment and into the field on the other side, an area used for parking. Roadways had already been marked out on the rough turf with chalk for the football season. Again, other than empty beverage cans, yellowing newspapers, fading fast food containers, and the ubiquitous plastic bags caught in the stunted bushes on the edge of the field, nothing was found. The trash barrels near the entrances to the parking lot were empty, also. Pascoe look across the expanse of rough grass that extended for almost a half of a mile to the concrete and brick monolith, brightly colored flags now fluttering from tall poles on the exterior of the stadium. In a few days thousands of cars would jam into these fields, and tens of thousands would walk across them.

She slowly scanned the area a second time. She was hoping for that one substantial clue that could connect a shooter and a place. None materialized. She had the interns cover the area around the hedge a second time, the searchers now divided into teams and using metal detectors. Three crushed beer cans, a rusty railroad spike, a large bolt, and several nails were found before the single shell casing showed up. The brass casing was carefully removed from the tall grass and dropped into an evidence bag. Pascoe looked at the casing, 7mm. Using this as a teaching opportunity, she showed how to record where it was found on a map and how to label each piece of evidence. A second sweep of the area yielded several more metal objects, but no more brass.

Eventually Pascoe put Baker in charge of the interns as they began to sweep the left side of the railroad embankment with the metal detectors. She returned to Arden's condo and carefully extracted the bullet from the wall, dropped it into an evidence bag, adding a label to the bag's exterior. She locked the bags in the trunk of her car before starting the trek to Branch County.

34

On her way to Branch County, Pascoe stopped at the home of Elmer Jayson, the engineer who had witnessed the shooting and stopped the train. Jayson's house was just off the highway, its shape suggesting a style of farmhouse built in the early years of the century, but extensive additions and modernizations had been appended to the original footprint. Jayson saw Pascoe pull off the road and met her in the circular drive at the side of the house. He escorted her through a back entrance into the kitchen, a bright, airy room that occupied the addition that had been tacked onto the back of the house. Jayson's wife, a tall, pretty woman in her late fifties, served them coffee and then disappeared.

Pascoe pulled a recorder and note pad from her brief case. She placed the recorder on the table, keyed it on, and opened a pad to a new page.

Jayson pulled his glasses off and laid them on the table. He rubbed his eyes and put his glasses back on. He, like Pascoe, had been up most of the night.

After a few minutes of small talk, Pascoe began the interview. "I'll be going over the things you told me last night. This time I'd like to go slowly and make careful notes. It's most useful if you talk about what you saw in sequence."

He nodded his understanding as he started, "We bring the train down to limits before we get to the edge of town and then speed up when we get to the other side. I'm always extra careful when I run through the university. Seems like the train draws them. We've had suicides, drunks, even doped-up kids stumble onto the tracks. I've never hit anyone, and I don't want to."

"Last night I was just beginning to add power when I saw someone in the headlight. He's running toward me. I lay on the horn. Then I see a second person. It looks like he's following the first guy."

"Can you describe him, the first person?"

"Well, he was running fast, and I was speeding up. I don't know what you know about trains, but it takes a long time to get'em going and a long time to stop'em. I let go of the throttle and got ready to apply the brakes. I was mostly watching, hoping they'd stay off the tracks." He paused and stretched, arms back, then yawned. "The first guy was in black, all black."

"How about his face?"

"Face too. He had some kind of mask on. You know, like one of the knit things."

"Was it open around his eyes, nose, and mouth like a balaclava, or just holes like a ski mask?"

"I think it was more like the second, I couldn't see his face."

"Could you tell his color or race? Was he white, black…?

"No, I don't think there was much skin exposed. And everything happened so fast, the distances closing so quickly. He was carrying something. I could see it was a gun."

"What kind of a gun?"

"It wasn't a pistol. It was a long gun. You know, a shotgun or a hunting rifle."

"Can you remember anything specific about the gun?"

"Like?"

"Did it have a wood stock or one of those wire, folding kind of things. Did you see a scope?"

"I saw a gun, I can't tell you about that other stuff. I think it just looked like a normal kinda rifle, if you know what I mean. I was watching the guys, hoping they wouldn't try to cross the tracks at the last minute."

"How far apart were they?"

"Hard for me to judge, but I'd say a pretty good distance, fifty, sixty yards. Maybe more." Jayson yawned again, stretched and ran his hands over his gray brush-cut. He got up, got the coffee pot and refilled both their cups.

"Then what happened?"

"The first guy disappeared off to the side and I was looking at the second guy. I couldn't tell what he did. I had the brakes locked up by then. I was pretty sure I missed him.

After I got stopped, I slowly reversed back, hoping not to see his body on the tracks. And then I came down off the engine to look around. That's where I met you."

"Anything else you remember?"

"No, that's about all. I tried to stay out of the way, went back and stood by the locomotive. After I talked to you, I finished my run. Most nights are pretty boring, but occasionally you have something like this. Just never know what's going to happen."

Pascoe slid her card across the table. "If anything else occurs to you, please call."

"Sure will, Miss. Hope that guy's going to be all right."

"I hope so, too," she responded, giving him a weak smile as they shook hands.

35

Elkins was dreaming. He was falling backwards into a deep cave, out of control, spinning slowly. He stopped with a start and gazed into a heavy mist. He blinked, blinked again. The mist cleared, and he could see Dr. Kristin Gutiérrez leaning over the bed.

He heard her say, "I think we have someone waking up."

She was smiling and squeezing his right hand. "How are you feeling?"

"Not too good. Worst hangover of my life." He gave her a weak smile. "I thought you practiced painless medicine."

"I do. You're not my patient, yet. Unfortunately, you are still breathing. I don't get to peel your face back and find out what makes you tick, not this time anyway. This is Dr. Savage," she lifted her head to indicate the other side of the bed. Elkins looked up at the tall, balding man in blue surgical scrubs. Gutiérrez continued. "He's a neurologist, he spent most of the night monitoring your condition."

"Do you remember talking to me last night?" Savage asked.

"Sort of. Everything is a bit of a blur. I remember the bright lights and lots of people around me. How am I doing?" Ray asked, trying to pull the man into focus.

"Your CT scan is unremarkable. There's no skull fracture or evidence of bleeding. That said, sometimes things change, so we will want to hold on to you for the next 24 to 48 hours just to be on the safe side," said Savage looking down at him. "Before you were injured, what's the last thing you remember?"

"I remember running and a train, it's all sort of confused, like a dream after you wake up. You know, you're not sure what really happened, and it's all fading fast."

"So you don't remember falling, anything like that."

"No, not at all," Ray answered. "So what time is it now?"

"It's just after 11:00 A.M." Savage replied, pointing to a clock on the wall. "How's your vision? Can you see the clock clearly or is it blurred?"

"No blurring."

"Okay. Do you know what day it is?"

"Saturday," said Ray, after a short pause.

"Good. We're going to be monitoring you very closely."

"Anything else wrong with me?" he asked.

"You took a very hard fall. I'm surprised you didn't sustain any fractures. You were a mess when I first saw you, but you cleaned up okay. You have bumps and bruises. And once we get you up and around, you're going to have some aches and pains."

"I could use a cup of coffee."

"Not for the next few days," said Savage. "And after you're discharged, you are going to have to take it easy for a week or ten days. Lots of rest, plenty of fluids, no alcohol, and moderate exercise. Do you use tobacco?"

"No."

"Good. You're going to be on vacation for a week."

"I don't have time for this," said Ray.

"I hear that a lot," Savage replied.

"How about this headache?"

"I'll order some Tylenol. I don't want you to take any other pain meds. I'll have an office appointment scheduled for you at the time of your discharge. Do you understand?"

"Yes," answered Ray, repeating back what he had just been told.

"You need to rest and take it easy. I'll be back to check on you in a few hours."

Elkins watched him depart.

"And I've got to run, too," said Dr. Gutiérrez. "I've got several soccer games to officiate. Anything you need, magazines...?"

"How about this week's *New Yorker* and a tall cup of French roast."

"I'll get you the magazine. Coffee, you heard the man."

36

Branch County, seventy miles north of the university, was one of the most rural and economically depressed areas of the region. It lacked the rich soil that had brought prosperity to most of the state.

Pascoe parked in the visitors' lot at the front of the Branch County Sheriff Department, a single story, flat-roofed building covered in a pinkish brick. She could see the county jail immediately behind, an aging three-story stockade-like building of cement block and reinforced concrete with bar-covered windows.

She stopped at the switchboard. A deputy, a woman about her age, led Pascoe to Sheriff Mike Ney's office. The sheriff—short, heavy-set; bald except for a half-oval of gray hair; long sideburns; with a belly that hung over his belt—leaned forward over his desk to shake hands.

After settling into a chair, Pascoe said, "Thank you for coming in on a Saturday. I really appreciate it."

"No problem, Miss. In a small department we hardly notice what day of the week it is, there's always something that needs attending to. Sort of like having a dairy herd, if you know what I mean."

Pascoe nodded and smiled, unsure of what he was referring to.

"So, how's Elkins?" Ney asked.

"He had a serious concussion and has to stay in the hospital for a day or two for observation."

"Don't know him well, but I've heard several talks he gave at the Sheriff's Association meetings. Seems like a smart man, but practical, too. Not like some of those college people."

"Tell me about Merchant?" asked Pascoe, allowing his comment to pass.

"Well, I sent a couple of men to pick him up this morning, but he wasn't there. They questioned his grandfather, that's who he lives with. The old man is kinda senile. Can't remember when he last saw Arlin, but thought it was a day or two ago. I checked with his parole officer, guess he hasn't showed up for work in a week." He pulled his glasses off and looked across at Pascoe. "Course, that's not surprising. Whole family's alcoholics. Imagine he just wandered off to do some drinking. In a few days he'll run outta money and booze and come wandering back. What makes you think he might be involved in this shooting? You mentioned something about a letter on the phone."

"I've got a copy here." Pascoe sorted through her briefcase for a few moments and handed him a copy of the letter and the envelope, each in a plastic cover.

Ney put his glasses on to read the letter. He looked up at Pascoe and turned back to the letter. After he finished, he turned it over and set it on his desk. Then he examined the envelope. "The letter was sent from our post office, that's clear. But are you sure Arlin wrote this? I mean, it's obscene and all that, but it's a pretty good letter. I didn't think anyone in his family was educated enough to write this good."

"The woman who received this letter is a member of the English department. He was a student in two of her classes at the penitentiary. She's sure it's his handwriting."

"Letter's about sex, doesn't say anything about violence."

Pascoe didn't respond immediately. She took a deep breath and exhaled slowly.

"Can you tell me about Merchant, the kinds of crimes he's been involved in?"

"Pretty minor stuff, not in terms of the law, of course, but in real terms. Never heard him doing anything but stealing. When he was a kid, it was bikes and candy. By the time he was fifteen or sixteen, he was stealing cars, just joy riding at first. He got time in the juvie for that. Then he found out he could make some pretty good money by parting them out, better than the minimum wage jobs he was occasionally getting. He had a whole bunch of late model cars hidden back behind their garage in the woods. He was selling parts on order, sorta like a junk yard. If he didn't have a part someone wanted, he'd steal a car to get what he needed. That's what got him sent up. He had so many cars in that woods that someone couldn't help but notice. Don't think he ever used a gun or any other sorta weapon. Just steal cars at night. We think some of his friends were involved, too. We just never could nail them."

"Was he ever suspected of any sex offenses?"

"Far as I know, never." Ney paused. "In a little town like this everybody knows everyone else's business. I've known Arlin from the time he was a kid. That poor bastard never had a chance. Family's dirt poor, always has been. Never had the pot or the window, if you know what I mean. Arlin got most of what he needed from the time he was a kid by stealing. His people have always been trash. Merchant's mother got knocked up with him when she was fourteen or fifteen. No idea who the father was, guess every boy in these parts got some of her. She had one more kid, a girl, before she got killed."

"How did she die?"

"Car accident. Hit a tree. She was with some guy, both drunk. It was such a mess, never could quite tell which one of them was driving. Funny thing, on that whole stretch of road, bout two miles, there's only one tree, a big oak, rest's all fields. They hit the damn thing at seventy or eighty miles an hour. Must a been in a hurry for something." He gave her a sly smile.

"How about Merchant's sister?"

"She was a chip off the old block. She got in trouble while still a kid. A year or two later she met some guy and moved away. Don't think she's ever been back." He picked up the letter and looked at it again. "Sending a letter like this ain't right, but it ain't illegal, either. And the letter don't say nothing about shooting her."

Pascoe looked at him, her eyes burning into him. "The things he's suggesting are felonies."

Ney pushed back from his desk. "Has he bothered this woman? Has she seen him? Has he been hanging around? Has he been stalking her?" His tone suggested annoyance.

"No, I don't believe so. Just the letter."

"Well, Miss, we'll keep looking, and we'll pick Merchant up for questioning when we find him. But I don't think Arlin is the person you're looking for." He extended his hand without getting up, indicating to Pascoe that the meeting was over.

37

~~~~~~~

Elkins spent a restless day, bothered by a nagging headache and fatigue. By late morning one of the nurses had him up and walking, at first a challenge, every muscle in his body crying out in pain. He felt better after showering and fell into an uneasy sleep that absorbed most of the afternoon. When he next opened his eyes, Charlene Pascoe was at his side. As he worked to pull himself to full consciousness, he asked, "What time is it?"

"It's just after five."

Elkins was suddenly fully awake. "Arden, is she all right?"

"Not bad. Shaken by the events, and she needed some stitches to close a cut. She spent last night here. Now she's staying with your neighbors, the Chestertons. Mrs. Chesterton picked her up midday. I explained the situation to Jack Kackmeister. He has promised to keep their house under close surveillance."

Elkins rubbed his eyes with his left hand. "I'm glad you're here, I was thinking about the things I needed to tell you, things I should have written down." Carefully, he recounted his conversation with Jane Arden. "Have you learned anything about Arlin Merchant?"

"I went out to Branch County and talked with Mike Ney, the sheriff. Do you remember him, looks to be in his late sixties, short, and fairly stout?"

"Yes."

"I called his office this morning. He wasn't in, but I talked with the shift commander. I told him about the shooting and asked if they would pick up Merchant for questioning. I drove out there without confirming that they had taken him into custody. I needed something to do. I can't stand sitting around and waiting. As it turns out they couldn't find him. According to his parole officer, Merchant hasn't shown up for his job for a week."

"Did you find out anything?"

"Ney gave me the history of the Merchant clan. I don't think that you would call it a completely unbiased history. I showed him a copy of the letter. He was impressed by its literary quality. Long and short of it is he doesn't think Merchant is our man. Says Merchant's a thief, but this shooting is out of character with the Arlin Merchant he knows."

"What do you think?"

"I don't know. I've looked at his arrest record. His problems with the law involve alcohol, stealing cars, and selling off parts. There's no mention of his ever having a weapon of any kind in his possession. And there's no record of sex offenses or drug possession. He was in the juvenile system by the time he was fourteen. He's gone to trial twice for motor vehicle theft, the first time he got off because he wasn't Mirandized. Ney didn't mention that fact. The second time Merchant wasn't as lucky. He got three to five, did the minimum. I've got his records. He was a model prisoner and earned 21 hours of college credit."

Pascoe looked over at Ray. His attention seemed to be flagging. "Elkins, can you answer some questions, or are you getting too tired?"

"I'll try to stay awake. I'm really exhausted, and I have a headache."

"I got a statement from Jane Arden this morning. I need to go over the same ground with you."

"Where do you want me to start?"

"Arden said that you arrived about 9:00 P.M."

"I'm not sure it was that late, but it was at least 8:30. I think I had told her I would be over about 6:00, but I was running late. I called and suggested that perhaps I should come by another time, but she wanted me to look at the locks, and she offered me dinner. I checked the locks and told her what needed to be done. She was making dinner. The storm hit about the time we were sitting down. The lights went out, but she had some candles going. I remember the breaking glass, pushing her to the floor, and calling for help. I went out the patio door. I thought I saw someone sprinting along the hedge at the back of the complex. I took off after them. Then there was a locomotive and then everything gets very jumbled."

"Can you remember anything about the person you were chasing?"

"I can remember the brilliant light of the locomotive and a figure. It was almost like a shadow."

"Tall, short, fat, thin, male, female?"

"Don't know about the sex, but I would say tall and thin. That's only an impression. Maybe you should interview Oscar Miller."

"Who's that?" pressed Pascoe.

"He's the tenured medievalist in the English Department. He's supposed to be a very unpleasant person."

"What connection does he have to this case?"

"No connection at all, far as I know. Just something I was planning to do."

"Oscar Miller. Okay, I'll have a talk with him. What am I supposed to ask him?"

He shook his head. "You'll think of something. And see what you can find out about Jane Arden." Then he closed his eyes.

38

Early Monday morning Pascoe called Oscar Miller to arrange a meeting. There was no answer at his office number and no home listing in the faculty and staff directory. Then she called Alice Widdowson, Clifford Chesterton's secretary, who provided her with a home number for Miller.

Later that morning at 11:00, Pascoe stood outside Miller's third floor office door in Old West Foundation Hall. The door was closed. She could hear movement in the office and knocked. The door opened a crack and a wizened visage peered out at her.

"Miss Pascoe?"

"Yes."

The door was opened farther, and she was ushered in and offered a chair. She was surprised by how short Miller was; she guessed that he was barely five feet tall. His head, compared to the rest of his frame, was disproportionally large. His long, gray hair was combed back. His face—nose, long, thin, pointed, with large nostrils that opened forward; forehead, sloping back to his hairline at an angle almost as steep as his nose; and chin, small, and dropping back from the line of his upper jaw—reminded her of the drawing of a weasel in one of her childhood books. His eyes, light blue, darted nervously back and forth.

After a few minutes of small talk, Pascoe explained what kind of information she was seeking. "Professor Miller, as you know, one of your colleagues, Jane Arden, had an attempt made on her life Friday night. We're trying to develop a list of possible suspects in this case. Perhaps you could help us."

"Why ask me?" scoffed Miller. His breath reeked of tobacco.

Pascoe thought it was a good question. She was interviewing Miller because Elkins had asked her to, but she wasn't sure why. *How should I play this?* Pascoe thought, She glanced around Miller's office. The two side walls were covered with bookcases. Two bumper stickers were pinned to the top corners of a bulletin board.

"I like your bumper sticker," she said.

"Which one?"

She pointed to the one on the left, *Support Your Local Police.* "We need more of that. We really appreciate citizen support." Pascoe hoped that she didn't sound too insincere. She didn't comment on the bumper sticker on the right, *This is a Republic, NOT a Democracy.* "That's why I'm talking with you. We don't have any good leads on why anyone would want to kill Professor Arden. We're asking members of the faculty, especially members of your department, for help. Since you and Arden share the same specialty, I hoped perhaps you might have some thoughts on the matter."

"Frankly, Miss Pascoe, strange as it sounds, I barely know Miss Arden. I don't know anything about her personal life, and I don't know why anyone would want to kill her."

"How about her professional life?"

"Don't know much about that either. She did her work in Ann Arbor, which isn't the best place for studies in our field. That said, she's a real expert in Old English. But, I was never asked to take part in her interview, or in any of the others, either."

"Which others?"

"The other medievalists in the department: Bensen, Hendrickson, Dalton. We never needed those people. They were all second rate."

"What are you telling me?"

"Bensen, for instance. Her dissertation was very pedestrian. She wrote on minor women writers of the late medieval period." He continued in a mocking tone, "She didn't have much to work with, and those writers would have been best left forgotten. It was the women's thing, that's what got her through. Her dissertation should have been rejected, but she cowed her committee. Damn feminists have everyone scared. Bensen tried to do the same thing here with her tenure. Good thing the department stuck to its guns.

"The thing you need to understand, Miss Pascoe, is there isn't much enrollment in this area. I can barely get a load. Even before the others were hired, I often had to teach undergraduate survey courses in English literature."

"How about Hendrickson, what kind of scholar was she?"

"She might have been a scholar, but her area of scholarship wasn't literature. She was an authority on bourbon whiskey, not much else. And that was all experiential learning rather than book learning, if you catch my drift. She got hired because her father and our former chair were friends during their undergraduate days at Charlottesville. The woman was always half smashed, and she wasn't much of a medievalist. Her dissertation had a title like *The Resonances of Latin Rhetoric in English Medieval Literature.* Her real interest was classical rhetoric, not medieval literature."

"How about Dalton?"

"Dalton was a fairly adequate scholar. Her real interest was the stories conveyed by medieval stained glass, the windows of the great cathedrals. She really should have been in art history, not in English."

"I'm impressed by how much you know about their dissertations."

"I did the necessary legwork." He held her in his gaze and continued sternly, "If you don't have any say on who's going be hired, you've got to make it your business to find out about them." Miller got up and went to the bookcase that covered the wall opposite his desk. He removed four paperbacks from the far side of the bottom shelf. The books had identical light blue covers, and a title printed on a label and attached to the front. He handed the volumes to Pascoe. "These are their dissertations. I ordered copies from University Microfilms. I also have copies of all their published articles." He motioned toward a metal file cabinet. "When they were hired I used the old boy network, people I knew at the schools they came from, to find out as much as I could about each of them. I was even able to get some of their former office mates on the phone." He pointed the index finger of his hand at Pascoe and repeatedly gestured to emphasize his point. "If I were going to have to deal with these women, I had to know about them. I especially wanted to know if they were leftist."

"And?" she asked, feigning interest.

"None were in really hard-core leftist groups, but Bensen was involved in that radical feminist stuff, which I think is about as subversive as you can get. She had that socialist, lesbo world-view. At faculty meetings she'd launch into these long diatribes on how the canon had to be changed, that we were just teaching the works of dead white men. She kept haranguing us about how we had to include women writers and the works of people of color. What she could never get through her head was that if these people had written anything worthwhile, we would be teaching them. It's not like we're prejudiced or exclusionary. These feminists don't understand that women lack the same intellectual power. That's why there aren't women Chaucers, or Shakespeares, or Miltons. That's why all the great chefs are male. That's why all the great actors are male. It's a truth they just can't accept."

Pascoe kept writing in her notebook, trying not to respond.

"The point I'm making is we shouldn't have hired them. They all got their jobs by conniving, by making out that they were something they were not. They weren't world-class medievalists, not one of them. And they're all Catholic, did you know that?"

"No, I didn't. The way you said that suggests there is something else I should know."

"They were all in that parish run by that Jesuit priest. I think he calls himself Father Bob. You know about the Jesuits?" He pointed with his left index finger again, gesticulating three times as he slowly pronounced "Jesuits."

"No, I don't know much about Catholicism."

"They're a communist front organization from way back," he proclaimed angrily. "They pretend to be a religious order. I have it on good authority that the Jesuits are headed by a bunch of Jews, all connected with the Rothchilds and George Soros. The Pope is in on it, too. They've organized resistance movements all over Latin America. We've been lucky that anti-communist generals down there have kept these bastards from taking over the whole damn region. Both Castro and Che Guevara were trained by the Jesuits."

"I'm really impressed by how much you know on a variety of topics," said Pascoe with schoolgirl awe. The conversation was going exactly in the direction she had hoped. "Is there anything else that I should know about?"

"I don't know about Arden, but the other three women were queer. I guess I should call them lesbians. I'm the only one in the department who has the courage to call a spade a spade, the hell with political correctness." Miller fell into a bout of coughing. He pulled a green glass bottle from a bottom drawer, opened it, and took several swigs. "Cough medicine," he said. "Only thing that works."

"It would be helpful if you could tell me how you acquired this information," asked Pascoe, the air now filled with the scent of brandy. "Well, first, years ago when they were just new here, I asked both Bensen and Hendrickson out. Just as I suspected, they both refused me. I could tell they didn't like men. And they were all involved in that radical feminist group, Sisters for a Shared Future." He leaned closer to Pascoe and said in a low voice. "I have it on good authority that they're all lesbians, all of them. They won't let you in if you're not."

"Do you know if any of these women had enemies in the English Department or anywhere else in the university?"

"I can think of one person."

"Who?"

"Seneca Carducci, our Negro, black lit, Miltonist homosexual."

"Why?"

"Well, don't you know," Miller said in a tone that suggested that he was repeating a universal truth, "Queers always hate lesbians. It's probably just self-hate, a transference of sorts. They are disgusted by the other's perversion. Not that I take much stock in that Freudian stuff, but it clearly applies here."

"That's interesting," said Pascoe innocently, "I didn't know that. Professor Miller, you've been very helpful. Thank you so much for your time."

"Glad to help, Miss Pascoe. Like that sign says, I'm always glad to help the police."

39

Pascoe was able to unwind from her encounter with Oscar Miller on the long ride to Branch County. Once there one of the deputies guided her through security to the jail's interior. She waited for Merchant inside the interview room, a small, windowless cubicle with an oak table and four gray steel chairs. Feeling claustrophobic, Pascoe moved out to the hall while Merchant was brought from a holding cell. She caught a glimpse of him as he was being led down the hall. When he was seated across from her—Ney on her right, and a deputy leaning against the wall next to the door—she was able to observe him more closely.

Although she knew Merchant to be in his twenties, as he sat across from her, he looked much older. He had a four or five day beard, and his long, ragged, unwashed hair hung almost to his shoulders. He was unkempt, grimy, and he stank of tobacco, booze, and filth. He sagged in the chair, his head down, mouth open.

Ney, looking toward the microphone on the side of the table near the wall, stated the time and date, identified the people in the room and asked Merchant to state his full name. Without looking up, Merchant mumbled his name.

Ney pointed to the microphone. "Microphone is over here, Arlin. You gotta speak in a clear voice or the recording sounds like a bunch of mumbo jumbo."

Merchant lifted his head and gave Ney a hostile sneer. "Arlin Lee Merchant."

As he spoke, Pascoe could see Merchant was missing several teeth. The rest were mottled with large areas of decay.

Ney asked, "Arlin, when you were taken into custody, were you read your rights?"

"Ya."

"Before this interview, were you given the right to be represented by counsel?"

"Ain't got nothing to hide. Don't need no fucking lawyer."

"Arlin, according to the people over at the county garage, you haven't been in since last Tuesday. Where have you been?

"Don't know."

"What do you mean, don't know?"

"Can't remember much bout the last few days."

"Well," said Ney, finding humor in Merchant's response, "tell us what you can remember."

"Sunday," he paused, "maybe it was Monday, Kenny comes over. Kenny's got more than a thousand bucks. He shows me the money and says we should celebrate."

"Where in the world did Kenny Nelson ever come up with a thousand dollars?" Ney asked.

"He got it from his brother, Donny, the lawyer."

"Donny gave him a thousand dollars?"

"No, it's from a law suit. Kenny fell and busted his two front teeth outside the Farwell Tap couple a years ago. Donny sued them for Kenny. Got the settlement check from an insurance company on Monday. Donny took half and gave Kenny a thousand. He's holding on to the rest of the money for Kenny."

"So what did you and Kenny do?"

"Kenny wanted to go on a road trip. We went and got five, six cases of beer and a case of Jim Beam. Kenny said something about going to Tucson to see Doug. Sounded good to me, ain't never been to Tucson. Went back to Kenny's, and that's as far as we got till we ran out of beer, maybe Friday or Saturday. Kenny went and got some more."

Ney looked over at Pascoe, turning the questioning over to her. "Did you go anywhere after you got to Kenny's?" she asked.

"Not till last night. Kenny wanted me to help him take the empties back."

"Were you in University Center this week?" asked Pascoe.

"Where?"

"University Center."

"No, ma'am."

"Is there anyone who can verify your story?"

"Kenny."

"Is there anyone besides Kenny?"

"No, ma'am."

Pascoe opened a folder and placed a copy of a letter on the table in front of Merchant. "Did you write this letter?"

Merchant leaned forward, extended a grimy finger and pulled the sheet closer to him. He peered at the page for a long moment and said, without looking up, "Yeah, I wrote it. Ain't no law bout writing letters."

Before Pascoe could ask her next question, Ney said, "This isn't the kind of thing you send to a lady." In a scolding tone he added, "You know better than that, Arlin. Think you would a gotten paroled if the board knew what kind of letters you sent?"

"Let me ask you this question again," said Pascoe. "Were you in University Center this week?"

"No."

"Mr. Merchant, have you been in University Center since you've been released from prison?"

"No, ma'am. I think I was only there once. That was a long time ago."

"What was your intent when you," she stopped mid-sentence and rephrased her question. "Why did you write this letter?"

"I was mad."

She softened her tone. "What were you mad about?"

"When I was in her class, she was real nice to me. After I got out of her class, I wrote her a couple of letters, and she wrote back. I wrote her a couple more times, but she didn't write back. Then Zeigler tells me I ain't to write her any more. I don't, don't till I get out. Then I wrote her this because I was pissed. Thought it would scare her a bit."

Pascoe continued in the same tone, "What were you angry about?"

Merchant didn't answer immediately; he continued to look down. He lifted his head slightly and looked at Pascoe. "She was just like all the rest. They come and teach their class and treat you real nice, like you're a real person and all that. But it's all fake, a bunch of bull. You're dirt. You know it, and they know it."

Pascoe looked over at Ney. "I don't have anything else."

"Okay, Bob," said Ney. The deputy escorted Merchant out.

"What now?" she asked.

"He's almost sober. We'll feed him some coffee and peanut butter sandwiches and give him a ride home. He's his parole officer's problem now."

"Any chance I could talk to Merchant's alibi, Kenny Nelson?

"I could probably arrange that, but he'll insist on having his brother in the room. He's the sleaziest lawyer in the county. I'll make some phone calls. I'll be back in a few."

Pascoe was keying her notes into her laptop when Ney returned.

"Well, it's not going to happen today. Donny is taking a deposition this afternoon and is unavailable, but I'm sure we can get Donny to cooperate."

"Why are you so sure? You said he was a real sleaze."

"We found something else in the car, a bag of grass, less than an ounce. I'm sure Donny will be real helpful if I suggest we might be able to work something out."

"You didn't find a rifle in Kenny's car by any chance?"

Ney looked amused, "Now Miss Pascoe, if we'd found a gun, I would have told you right off."

"Any chance of searching Kenny's house? I'm just trying to explore all possibilities."

"Getting a search warrant would be a lot of trouble. We kinda do things informal here when we can. I'm sure I can have Donny go with me and look around his brother's house. He'll be real helpful. He won't want his brother involved in a felony."

As Pascoe drove back to University Center, she remembered Elkins's counsel to put herself in the other person's world. She thought about Merchant's world. It happened all the time, inmates falling in love with women who work in prison programs. On the inside they're separated by guards, bars, and walls. On the outside they're separated by social class and education. Pascoe understood his rage.

40

~~~~~~~

Pascoe arrived in the late afternoon carrying a large brown paper bag. Ray could smell the curry as soon as he opened the door for her.

"What's going on?" he asked.

"You said you couldn't have coffee or wine, but you didn't say anything about spices. And I know how much you love Indian. And after a couple of days of hospital food, this is the least I can do for a friend."

"How about Merchant?"

"We'll talk about him over dessert. I don't want the food to get cold."

With Ray's help, Charlene got the table set and the food into serving containers. After they started eating, he said, "I've been held almost incommunicado for days. What's happened?

"Just the usual fun-filled fall weekend on campus. Some members of the hockey team duked it out with some lacrosse players over at the Candlelight Inn on Saturday night. It was a major brawl."

"What was that all about?" asked Ray.

"According to the best information I have, a member of the women's tennis team." Charlene laughed, "In your absence, I had calls from the chancellor's office, the A.D., and the hockey and lacrosse coaches."

"How about the women's tennis coach?" asked Ray.

"It appears that the tennis player left with a basketball player just as the fists began to fly."

"What's the outcome?"

"No one is interested in pressing charges and the owner of the Candlelight says there were no damages."

"Anything else?"

"No, thankfully. An unusually quiet weekend."

As they were clearing away the dishes, Elkins said, "Now can I ask about Merchant?"

"I am amazed, Ray. I didn't know that you could stay off task for this long. Bravo! Now here's the story. At the time they were picked up, both Merchant and the guy he was with, a fellow by the name of Kenny Nelson, had astronomical blood alcohols. Merchant said they had been drinking for six days, and by the length of his beard and his odor...."

"Bet you had to interview him in a little room with no ventilation?"

"You got it. Anyway, his story is that his friend, Kenny, got a grand from a damage suit, and the two of them dedicated themselves to drinking up the money. They were arrested when they came out for more beer."

"Any support for his alibi?"

"His friend, an equally disreputable person, seems to be the only one who can substantiate his story."

"So he has no alibi?"

"He doesn't have a strong alibi, but I just don't think he's our man."

"Why's that?"

"I believe his story. You should have seen him. He was barely functioning. And he's a completely defeated human being. When he hadn't been drinking for a week, he could probably write that letter, but I don't think he would act on it."

"Support?"

"He would need a way of getting here."

"How about Kenny?"

"Kenny was drunk."

"He could have taken Kenny's car without Kenny even knowing it."

"I don't think it happened. He'd also need a rifle with a scope. There was no weapon."

"Where did they look?"

"In the car. Ney is going to check Nelson's house."

"Lots of places you could lose a gun between here and Branch County—ditch, river."

"It's not Merchant, Elkins. He's not the shooter. Merchant's just a poor lost soul. Arden is probably the first person who ever treated him decently. She's probably the only person who ever found anything worthwhile in him. Talk to Ney. Can you imagine growing up in a little town where everyone thinks you and your family are total losers. I'm sure that's the way he's always seen himself. While he's in the penitentiary he takes a couple of courses from an attractive woman who says something positive about his work, and more importantly, suggests that he has value as a person. He's the schoolboy who's fallen for his teacher. Merchant reaches out to this woman in the only way he knows. Unfortunately, his approach is very inappropriate. When he's rebuffed, he strikes out at her. But he only does it on paper."

Elkins looked amused, "My memory is that when we first looked at Merchant's letter, you said you liked to nail 'bastards like that.' Those were your words, or something to that effect. Now I hear this bleeding-heart," he gestured toward her, "telling me that poor Arlin is the victim of his environment. I'm confused. Perhaps my brain is still rattled."

"It's all your fault. Remember your dictum about trying to understand the perpetrator? That's all I was doing. And I think it really applies here."

"If we don't have a likely suspect, we have a real problem. And," he paused for a moment, "if this shooting is connected with the other deaths, we're dealing with someone who will try again to achieve his ends."

"I've thought of that," she responded.

"We need to continue to keep Arden out of circulation and see if we can move the investigation forward."

"I'll make sure that happens."

"How about Jane Arden?"

"I looked at her pre-employment background check in her HR file. Nothing. And I ran her name through NCIC, nothing.

"Tomorrow morning let's go back to the carillon. We've missed something. We need to start there."

"I thought you were supposed to take it easy?"

"I will. I want to be there with you."

Pascoe started to protest, but she was cut off by the arrival of Stephanie Chesterton and Jane Arden. They were standing on the back deck knocking on one of the double doors to the kitchen. Elkins, after greeting them, turned to Jane Arden and said, "We were just taking about you." He went on to explain their continued concern for her security, allowing Pascoe to fill in the details.

"I will cooperate completely. I really appreciate what you are doing."

"Now if we could just get the patient to cooperate," said Pascoe, pointing at Ray as she gathered up her things.

"What time are you picking me up?" he asked as she was heading toward the front door.

"10:00 A.M., not a minute before," she replied on her way out.

"I was going to ask you to dinner," said Stephanie, "but it appears that your colleague has taken care of that."

As Stephanie was talking, Ray was looking at Jane Arden. She was at ease, relaxed and smiling. He felt very attracted to her, and it unnerved him.

"Jane," he said, "other than us, did you show or discuss the Merchant letter with anyone else?"

"Stephanie and Jim Zeigler, the fellow at the prison."

"Anyone else?"

"No one."

"How are you doing? How's the hand?" he asked.

"The hand is healing. The stitches come out sometime next week. But the real question is how are you doing? I'm so sorry about what happened to you. You go above and beyond your job description, and your reward is to almost get killed." She gave him a warm smile. "And now it's your turn to answer."

"I feel fine, I just miss my coffee. I'm suffering from caffeine withdrawal."

"How about pain?" asked Stephanie, entering the conversation.

"A few aches and pains, nothing really," said Ray.

"He needs a few weeks up in Michigan walking the beaches or kay-aking. That would bring a rapid recovery," Stephanie explained. "It would be a good time to be there," agreed Ray. "The weather is still warm and most of the tourists are long gone. The beaches are empty, and you can find a table in your favorite restaurant."

41

Pascoe was back in her office by 7:00 P.M. when Seneca Carducci, dressed in a black linen suit, black shirt, and a white tie, arrived. She greeted him and offered him a chair.

"Professor Carducci, I really appreciate you coming in, especially in the evening. We're trying to finish up the investigation on Hendrickson's death, and there are a few details I want to check on again. I'll probably go over some of the same material I covered last time."

"I thought everything was over with."

"It really is. There are just some odds and ends I'm still curious about. Last time we talked you suggested that Hendrickson was," she paused as she looked for the appropriate phrase, "involved in relationships with a number of people."

"That she was," he responded in a rich baritone voice. "She was a female Walt Whitman, without the gift, of course." Carducci rolled his eyes at Pascoe.

"Were there any women she was particularly close to, women she might have been having, let us say a romantic or sexual relationship with?"

"What time period are you asking about, the time of her death or the last two or three years?"

"Let's start with the time of her death."

"This past year she was involved with a doctoral student. She was on his committee. Fellow's name is Josh Lord, teaches at some backwater community college. Lord's a young stallion, pretty young wife, used to bring her and two sweet little kids into the office with him occasionally. I think he was just dicking Bobby Jo to get his dissertation accepted. He defended at the end of spring term. I don't think he's been around since."

Pascoe made a note on Josh Lord. "The last time we talked, you indicated that she might have been involved with some women. Do you know if she was involved with anyone in the English Department?"

"Ms. Pascoe, she was involved with a lot of people."

"Was there anyone in particular, that's what I'm trying to find out."

"And what I'm trying to tell you is that Bobby Jo was intimate with lots of folks, but close to no one. She was more like some men, if you know what I mean."

Pascoe shook her head, "I don't know what you mean."

"She separated sex from relationships. Sex was sex, and relationships were relationships. Few women do that, it's always about the relationship. I believe it has something to do with testosterone levels or that maternal thing."

Pascoe persisted, "Let me ask the question again. Do you know if there was a woman she was especially close to, or a woman who wanted to be close to her?"

Carducci rubbed his chin with the fingers of his right hand. "Last year Barbara Castlemain seemed to hang around a lot. I think she was doing a divorce at the time. If they had a thing going, I think Bobby Jo probably dropped her for Josh. He was cute."

"Did Professor Hendrickson have any enemies, people who might have been offended by her lifestyle, people who might have wanted to do her harm?"

Carducci got a broad grim. "Lot's of folks were probably offended by her lifestyle. Hey, this ain't Kansas, Dorothy, but it's close. Way close."

"Seriously," Pascoe heard her voice. It was the one she used on her younger brother when he was irritating her. She modified her tone, "Was there anyone who...."

"I don't think so. She was bizarre, but she was also warm and funny. Everyone in the department liked her. Even our crypto-Nazi seemed to have the hots for her at one time."

"Who is that?" Pascoe asked, already writing down the answer.

42

～～～

Promptly at 10:00 on Tuesday morning Pascoe pulled into Elkin's drive. He was waiting at the front door. As they drove across campus, she gave him a summary of her conversation with Seneca Carducci. She concluded by saying, "What a collection of characters."

"They are that," he agreed as they walked toward the carillon. The area was alive with activity. Students, most with backpacks, some on bikes and skateboards, filled the sidewalks near the carillon. A few sat on the widely spaced granite benches on the outer ring of cement walks that bordered the area or lounged on the lawns under the warm, morning sun. "Is there a killer in that crowd?"

"What's our plan?" asked Pascoe, not responding to Ray's question.

"I just want to walk through this, try to reproduce what Bensen might have done," said Ray. "We'll start with you unlocking the door."

Ray watched Pascoe contend with the old lock on the carillon door. It took her several attempts to finally get the key to turn in the cylinder. After she had the door unbolted he said, "Lock it again, will you?"

Pascoe locked the door.

"Now open it with your left hand."

Pascoe struggled with the lock until she was finally able to successfully manipulate the cranky mechanism. As she held the door for him, she gave him a knowing look. "Not something you would do if you were right handed."

"Did you check on whether Bensen was left handed?"

"I talked with her office mate, Barbara Castlemain. She said she was positive that she was right handed."

"Let's take our time and walk through this," he said.

Pascoe pulled the door shut; they stood for a minute and allowed their eyes to acclimate to the cool, dark interior.

"Time?" asked Ray.

"Ten-twenty."

"Bensen jumped or was dropped at about ten," he said. "This is about what the place would have looked like. Would you have turned on the lights if you were Bensen or someone carrying Bensen?"

"It's pretty gloomy in here, but if you took a couple minutes for your eyes to adjust, there's enough light from the windows to walk to the stairs with safety."

"And the lights were off when you came in here the first time?"

"Yes."

"Let's climb the stairs."

"Are you going to be able to do this?"

"I am perfectly okay."

"But you are not to exert yourself."

"We'll go very slowly." Elkins stopped at the first landing. "If you were Bensen on your way to kill yourself, what would you be thinking?"

"That's a hard question. You're asking me to logically explain the thoughts of an irrational person."

Elkins shook his head and made an affirmative hum.

"I guess if I were going to do this, I would be thinking that this act would really show those dirty bastards who didn't give me tenure," said Pascoe. "I would think that I was laying the ultimate guilt trip on them. I might even see this as a romantic gesture, something that would make me a martyr of sorts. From what we've heard, Bensen was passionate about her beliefs."

Elkins stopped on the next landing to catch his breath. "And if you were her killer?"

"I think he...."

"He?" Ray asked.

"Look at these stairs. I'm assuming that she would be unconscious. It would take a strong person to carry her up these stairs. So it would be either a ripped man or an Amazon woman."

"Why are you assuming that she was unconscious?"

"I don't know, it just seemed that...."

"I assumed that, too," said Ray, "but I may be changing my mind. Let's deal with that later. If you were the murderer you would...."

"Assumptions, assumptions. I'm assuming the killer is reasonably bright and thorough. He wants to make her death appear to be a suicide." She added as an aside, "Something that he has succeeded in doing." She paused and waited for Elkins at the next landing. "I'd want to make sure that the only prints were hers. I'd want to make sure that I could get in and out of here without being seen, and I'd want to make sure I didn't have any trouble with her. Wouldn't want the autopsy to show injuries that couldn't be attributed to the fall."

When they reached the upper level, Elkins said, "Continue."

"Again, it depends. If she were unconscious, I'd just need to push her through the window, putting her prints on the chair and key first. And I'd leave the chair under the window to give the impression that's how she climbed up."

"The prints on the chair?" asked Elkins.

"Left hand. That may be a careless mistake."

"Careless, but natural. We'll assume our killer is left-handed. After she goes out the window, what would you be concerned with?"

"Getting out of here and not being seen."

"How would you do that?"

"The window faces east, the door is to the west. Given the confusion during the first few minutes after she fell, he might be able to slip out the door and not be noticed. Or he might try to wait until the excitement was over, but that wouldn't be safe because sooner or later we would be coming into the building."

"Let's go down to the ground level," said Elkins. "What would the killer be feeling as he made this walk?"

"It depends. He might be in an absolute panic, or if he thinks that his ruse is undetectable, he might be feeling confident—mission completed and all that kind of stuff. But he still had to get away without his presence engendering any suspicion."

When they reached the ground floor, Elkins switched on the lights, knelt, and with his right hand grasped the corner of a large threadbare, oriental rug that was centered in the room. He pulled the rug off to the side. They gazed at the slate flooring covered with a fine layer of grit that had filtered through the carpet. He pulled the rug back to its original position and grabbed the opposite corner. A little more than a foot from the edge was a steel door, hinged at one side and level with the rest of the floor.

"You knew this was here," said Pascoe.

"I thought it was possible."

"Where does it go?"

"There are tunnels that run to all the buildings on central campus. Most of the mechanical systems are run through them—steam pipes, electric lines, phones and cable lines. The first time we were here, I wasn't thinking murder. But I've had several strange dreams the last few days. I just suddenly saw the whole thing."

"And you know who the killer is?"

"No. I just know that he had a way to get in and out without anyone seeing him, or her."

Pascoe bent down and looked at the door closely. "Doesn't seem to open from this side."

Elkins studied the door. "The lock must be in the tunnel. You would push it open into this room from down there," Ray pointed in the direction of the door. "We'll have to talk with John Stockton in maintenance and get a map of the system. We need to find out where you can enter the tunnels and not be seen."

43

John Stockton, the director of building and grounds, laid the blueprint out on a large drawing board that backed up against the steel-framed windows of his office. He swung a fluorescent lamp over the board and pushed the red button on the top. The twin bulbs flickered, then glowed.

"Sorry the map's such a mess," he said. "When the tunnels were first dug, sometime in the twenties when the original powerhouse was built, they were designed to carry only steam pipes and electrical cables. Then phone lines and extra power and steam lines were installed as new buildings were constructed. In recent years, cabling from the West Campus Computer Center has been added. The tunnels on central campus are seven feet tall and nine feet wide. Sounds big, but there's so damn much stuff down there these days you can hardly move. We've drawn in all the new additions to the prints, makes them awful busy looking. But," he pointed with his index finger, "if you follow these lines, you can pretty much see where the tunnels run. The double lines indicate the perimeters of the buildings."

"When we were in the carillon, it looked as though the door could only be opened from the tunnel side," said Ray.

"It's my understanding that originally that's how the system was designed. Probably wanted to make sure the students couldn't get in. I can remember when these doors didn't even have locks, just slide bolts on the tunnel side. The whole system had to be changed about twenty years ago when we had an electrical fire in one of the tunnels and there was no way to get easy access to the area."

"How was it changed?" asked Pascoe.

Stockton pointed to an area enclosed in a rectangle made by a red highlighter pen. "All the doors that can be entered from the surface are highlighted." He pointed out several more. "We installed doors that can be unlocked from either side at the end of every run. Then, as we get the funds, we're slowly replacing the rest of the doors. The door in the carillon is one of the few that hasn't been changed. It's probably the least used door in the system."

"These are keyed...."

"With the AU001 keys." said Stockton.

"Are maintenance people in the tunnels on a regular basis?" asked Ray.

"One of our guys does a walk-through once a week. He's just visually checking on things, replacing light bulbs. After we bring the heating system up every fall, usually about the middle of October, we inspect for leaks more often. Other than that, unless we're pulling wiring or cabling, there's seldom anyone down there."

"How about in the last few weeks, any work going on?"

"I don't think so, let me check."

Stockton went back to his desk and started reviewing schedules on his terminal. After he went through several screens, he said, "Just as I thought, nothing major scheduled. That doesn't mean a phone man or someone else hasn't been down there, but there was no major work scheduled."

"So," said Pascoe, "what you're telling us is that if someone had an AU001 key to gain access to the system, they could move from building to building with almost no chance of being seen."

"Most of the time, especially at night and on weekends," agreed Stockton. "Do you want to go down there and look around?"

"Yes," said Ray. "Where would we enter the system?"

"You can start at the power house, but it's real uncomfortable walking because you have to sorta bend down to keep from hitting your head on the pipe hangers. If you want to look at the access door below the carillon, you probably want to enter here," he pointed, "at West Foundation Hall or at Central Campus Engineering."

"Let's go in at Central Campus Engineering. I'd rather not have people in the English department see us snooping around the tunnel system," said Ray.

44

Stockton unlocked the steel door and pulled it open. He passed out hard hats to Pascoe and Elkins and donned one himself, "Watch your heads. There are lots of bolt ends below the pipe hangers."

As he waited for Stockton to close the door, Elkins looked down the tunnel. Steam pipes and electrical conduit hung from the ceiling and ran along both walls. The lights, bulbs in protective steel cages, formed luminous pools separated by areas of gray haze. The air was warm, dry, and stale.

Stockton squeezed past them and led the way, carrying a fiber-glass stepladder. Pascoe followed carrying an evidence kit. Ray was in the rear. They worked their way down the tunnel until Stockton stopped and turned to them, "You'll really have to watch your heads here, don't lose your hats." He bent down and moved into an alcove on the left side of the tunnel. The three of them could barely fit into it. Steel rungs protruded from the concrete to form a ladder to the trap door.

"What's the plan now?" Stockton asked, looking over at Pascoe.

"I'd like to dust these rungs for prints. I'll do the low ones first, and then with the ladder I'll get the higher ones and the latch."

Elkins and Stockton moved to the side as she began the process.

"Do you have enough light?" asked Stockton.

It's adequate," she responded. It took her a few minutes to check the lower rungs. Then she turned to Ray and said, "These have been carefully wiped. Should I do the rest?"

"Might as well, maybe the perp missed one."

Pascoe, with Stockton's help, maneuvered the ladder in place, checking the last two rungs and the handle on the trap door. When she finished, she looked down at Ray and said, "Nothing, not even a partial." She came down the ladder and stowed things back into the evidence case.

"What now?" asked Stockton.

"Let's get the ladder out of the way," said Ray. "Okay, now, John, I need to do some role playing. Would you go up the rungs and open the latch, and push that trap door open."

Stockton climbed up several rungs and carefully grasped the handle. "These old slide locks are a bitch to unfasten. They tend to rust tight." He struggled briefly to push the bolt back. "That wasn't too bad," he said, looking down at them. Then he started to push the steel door open. "Damn rug," he said under his breath, finally getting the door clear. "Go ahead and climb up into the carillon," said Ray.

Stockton peered down at them from the room above, his face framed in the light from below.

"Do you think you could do that while carrying a small, unconscious woman on your shoulder?"

"Only if I had first opened the door. Two trips. And then you'd have to be strong, athletic, and probably a lot younger than me."

Pascoe climbed up the ladder, Elkins observing from below. After a few minutes Stockton came down, followed by Pascoe. She pulled the door back, held it open with her head, and grabbed the rug, pulling it over the door before she lowered the door completely. They moved back into the main tunnel.

"What do you think?" asked Elkins.

"It wouldn't be easy, but it's possible," Pascoe responded.

Elkins turned to Stockton, "Can you show us the access door to West Foundation Hall?"

"It's the next one," Stockton said, leading the way. He stopped at a door where the tunnel made a ninety-degree turn to the left.

"What does the door open into?" asked Elkins.

"This one opens into a mechanical room. The real old buildings had their own boilers at one time. The boiler rooms became mechanical rooms after the powerhouse was built. Do you want to look around?"

"Yes," said Pascoe.

Stockton unlocked the door and they briefly examined the space and the adjoining hallway in the lower level of the building."

"So there's an entrance to this tunnel system in every building?" asked Char.

"Yes, you saw the map. It connects all the buildings on central campus. As you can see, the space is jammed. Seventy or eighty years of accumulation, work done by university employees early on, mostly outside contractors now, things done at different standards and codes. I don't have accurate mechanical plans for much of the older work. And I bet there's a ton of asbestos on the old pipes. It's a disaster waiting to happen. It should all be ripped up and replaced. But you know our budget, it will never happen," said Stockton. He led the way back to Central Campus Engineering.

"The sunshine feels good. I can't imagine working down there for any length of time," said Pascoe as they walked back to the patrol car. Once Pascoe was behind the wheel, she asked. "Do you want me to restate the obvious?"

"Go ahead, that's a major function in academic life."

"And in police work," she responded. "It would have been possible to use the tunnel system to get Bensen to the carillon undetected. If she were unconscious, the murderer needed to be strong enough to carry her. Climbing from the tunnel into the carillon would have been difficult, but doable. The perp took pains not to leave any prints. The key we found under the keyboard was probably just a plant to take us off the scent. Last, the perp could have gained access to the tunnel system from a lot of different buildings. The equipment rooms in most of them are in out of the way places. Unfortunately, we still don't have a suspect."

"We will," said Elkins. "Will you drive me to the office, please?"

"Shouldn't you be at home resting?"

"There must be a pile of paperwork that needs...."

"It's all taken care of," she said with a smile. "It's probably the first time anyone has ever been able to see the surface of your desk. I'm taking you home..."

"Here's the deal," said Elkins. "I'll go home now and take it easy for the rest of the day if you pick me up tomorrow morning. There are things that I need to get done."

Pascoe heard the earnestness in his voice. She decided that getting him to take the rest of the day off was a start. "You've got a deal. I'll pick you up at 8:00 A.M."

Elkins nodded and made an affirmative sounding groan.

45

Reda Rudd found Elkins on his back deck in a lounge chair reading a newspaper. He was startled by Reda's sudden appearance and not happy about having his privacy constantly invaded. "What are you doing here?" he asked.

"I went by the medical center, they said you were discharged yesterday. Then I went to your office and found Pascoe working at your desk. I asked where you were, and she said you were home resting. I promised her I wouldn't bother you."

"And you always keep your promises," said Ray, motioning toward an empty chair. "I'd offer you something to drink, but I don't know what's here. You might want to check the refrigerator."

She reached into her backpack and pulled out a Diet Coke. "I carry my own supply. I've got another one," she gave Elkins a questioning look.

"No, I can't do caffeine."

"I've got a lemon seltzer, too. It's warm, but I'll get you a glass with ice."

"That would be great," he said, reluctantly happy to be waited on.

When Reda returned from the kitchen, he asked, "Is this a social call, or are you collecting information for a *Daily* exclusive?"

"This is a social call. Pascoe has—I'm getting like you, just using last names—been keeping me informed on the investigation."

"The last name thing," said Ray, breaking in, "That's a bad habit, something I picked up in the military."

"Interrupting people is a bad habit, too," she flashed a smile. "Now listen, we've been running follow-up stories, but there hasn't been much to print. Besides, the killing and maiming of professors isn't of much interest to our readers. This week's major investigative report is on price-fixing by the local beer stores. We have to report on what's really important to our readers. However," she paused and gave him a waggish grin, "I'd be happy to learn about any new developments in the case. By the way," her tone changed, "I've started to get to know Pascoe the last few days. I like her. I can see why you hired her. She's a lot like you. But back to the topic, is there anything new?"

"About?"

"Let's start with the recent shooting. Are there any suspects?"

"Not at this time. We had one possibility, but he's no longer considered a likely suspect."

"Why were you at Professor Arden's townhouse? We printed what Pascoe told me, that you were there on routine police business."

"She was concerned about her door locks. I went there to check them."

Reda looked amused. "Come on Elkins, there has to be more to the story than that. You're too busy to be running around checking the locks on university-owned housing. Was she getting threatening calls or something?"

"I can't talk about it yet. Please be patient."

"If you can't, or more accurately won't, how about Bensen. Anything new there, or are we still doing suicide?"

Elkins was feeling uncomfortable. Their communication had always been open and without pretense, but there was a need not to let the murderer know they were starting to close in. "We're continuing to investigate."

"How long is that going to go on?"

"Until we can say with great certainty it was a suicide. If we end up thinking it was something other than suicide, we'll continue until we make arrests."

"How about Constance Dalton?"

"The same. Her death appears to be a suicide. We are still investigating. Reda, I believe our purposes would be best served if you would let this drop for a while. If these deaths turn out not to be suicides, I'll make sure you have all the information."

"Fair enough. But this is rather strange. I've been looking through the *Daily* archives. Not many faculty members kick off, at least until they're emeritus. Three people, one department...."

Ray inhaled deeply. "It is statistically improbable, Reda. That's why I'm going so slowly. I have to ask you to be patient. I promise you will have the full story."

"I trust you. I know you will," she said. "How are you doing?"

"Good. I should be back to normal in a few days. How about you?"

"Okay, mostly good. I think I'll be able to get my classes under control, and I'm feeling more confident about the new *Daily* staff than I was a few days ago."

Elkins looked at her, he had a hunch about something, but he wasn't sure how to approach the topic. "Do I remember you telling me about ending a relationship, or was that just one of my many dreams after my tumble?"

"No, that was real. It wasn't a long-term relationship. Right from the beginning I knew we had no real future."

"I didn't mean to pry into your private life...."

"Don't worry about it, no big thing. It was intense, sort of wild, but I don't need any more fucked-up relationships. The person I was in a relationship with, we couldn't even go out publicly."

"He's married or what?" asked Ray.

"It would have been clumsy. He's a priest."

Elkins leaned forward in his chair.

"Yeah, Father Bob at the campus religious center. I went to him for counseling, not that I'm much of a Catholic, but when you're having difficulty, you seem to wander back to your roots. One of my friends told me he was a great counselor, really able to help you get things into perspective fast." She looked over at Elkins. "I went to see him because I was really confused. I had gotten involved with someone in the history department—a man with a wife and three kids. It was the first time in my life that I felt my actions could hurt a lot of other people. I needed to talk it out. He helped me get out of that relationship, but we ended up as lovers."

"When did this all happen?"

"I first went in for counseling right before Christmas break. By the third or fourth session we were lovers. The first time right in his office, you know in the lower level of the religion c enter. He's got a couch in his office. It was wild. After that I'd meet him at his apartment. He'd call me when he was available. It went on for several months. Then one day he called me and said we had to talk. I met him at his office. He told me that he needed to end the relationship. He couldn't deal with the guilt anymore. He told me that he really loved me, but that he had committed his life to God, and that he couldn't stray from that promise. I didn't see him again until the night of the Chesterton party."

"How did you feel about that?"

"Well, at first I accepted it. It made good sense. I was impressed that he could overcome," her eyes crinkling, "the yearnings of the flesh and maintain his commitment—I have too many hormones in my system to ever consider celibacy. Then, you know how it is, something didn't seem right. I asked my friend, Kari—she's the one who recommended Father Bob—if she had ever been involved with him. She was embarrassed—she has trouble talking about sex—but admitted that she had a one-night stand with him. So I asked her, given that experience, how could she recommend him to me as a counselor? She said Father Bob told her that it had never happened before, and he didn't think that it would ever happen again. He gave her this line that there was something about her that awakened feelings he had never had before. I wonder how many women have fallen for this?"

Elkins poured some more seltzer into his glass.

"What do you think?" she asked.

"I've had limited contact with him. He seemed bright, sincere, and professional. Given his role as a counselor, his actions were totally inappropriate. So where are you now?"

"I say I'm okay, but I'm hurting. Even though I knew the whole thing was absolutely impossible, I really fell for him. But," she smiled, "someone new will come along. I haven't had any extended periods of celibacy since I was sixteen or seventeen."

Reda got up and pulled her backpack over one shoulder. "I've got to get back to campus. Is there anything I can help you with before I leave?"

"No, I'm fine, thanks."

She bent over and kissed him on the lips, a quick, playful kiss. "I like you, Elkins. Too bad you're so old. On the other hand, I'm sorta getting into old guys."

Elkins watched her go.

46

By early evening Elkins was napping on a couch in the living room. When he heard Stephanie calling, he tried to push the sleep away. When he finally opened his eyes, Stephanie was standing over him with a bottle of champagne in one hand and glasses in the other. Jane Arden was in tow. "Time to get up, Elkins." She popped open the bottle and started filling glasses.

"Stephanie," he protested, "No caffeine or alcohol. Doctor's orders."

"You're not having alcohol, you're having champagne. Did he say anything about champagne? Of course he didn't. This is medicinal, it gets your gastric juices going. I've made a wonderful dinner to celebrate your release, or shall I say escape, from the hospital.

The three of them settled around the kitchen table. Stephanie gave Elkins a half glass of champagne, filling her and Jane's glasses. When she had polished off her glass, she excused herself, saying she had to put the finishing touches on dinner. "Dinner is in thirty minutes. I expect you to be there on time."

After Stephanie left, Jane asked, "Given your last experience, do you feel comfortable sitting at the same table with me?"

"I was just thinking about that. How did you know?"

"Just had a feeling. Of course, you wouldn't have to be overly sagacious to make that leap. And," she laughed, "for all you know, I may be having the same feelings. The only time people ever shoot at me is when I'm with you."

"How much did Pascoe tell you about Merchant?" Elkins asked.

Jane could read his face. He was back in an investigative mode. "She gave me a thorough briefing. I understand why Merchant isn't a strong suspect. She also questioned me very extensively. I don't think I was able to help much."

"Anything occur to you since you talked with her? If Merchant wasn't the shooter, we're not left with much."

She sipped the rest of her champagne, refilled her glass and held the bottle toward Elkins's glass. He shook his head and covered the glass with his hand.

"I've thought about it a lot," she said. "I thought about old boy friends, former students. I don't remember anyone being really angry with me. People don't react that way toward me. I just can't think of anyone. Could it have been a random event?"

"Well," Elkins twisted in his chair trying to find a more comfortable position, but his discomfort was intellectual as well as physical, "that's always a possibility, but an unlikely one."

"Maybe they shot at the wrong house," she offered.

"Again, a possibility."

"But your tone suggests that it's fairly improbable."

"Let me ask you this, is there any possibility that you might have told someone else about the Merchant letter?"

Jane shook her head. "I told you, I told Stephanie, Zeigler at the prison. That's it."

"There's no chance that you might have mentioned it to anyone else. You must have talked to people about the deaths of your colleagues. Perhaps you just alluded to it in passing?"

"I talked to lots of people about those deaths. Let me think. Stephanie, Chesterton, Gus, and Father Bob...."

"Tell me about Father Bob. How do you know Father Bob?" asked Ray, suddenly alert and totally focused on their conversation. "I'm pretty much a fallen-away Catholic, but I do make it to mass a couple of times a year. And when my mother died, he was very helpful."

"How's that?"

"He's a very skilled counselor, very empathic. Among other things, he does grief counseling. And he was the appropriate person for me to talk to. I had mixed feelings toward my mother, especially when I was a teenager. After she died there were things I felt guilty about, conflicts that we had never resolved.

She was a devout Catholic, and I think much of my proclaimed agnosticism, especially when I was a teenager, was a way of getting at her. Father Bob was able to help me work through my feelings."

"How long were you in this, ah, counseling relationship?"

"About six months."

"During that time, was there," Elkins paused, trying to find a subtle way to phrase the question, "any behavior by Father Bob that was different than you expected?"

"What do you mean?"

"Did Father Bob ever show any interest in you as a woman, interest that exceeded what's usually appropriate in a client, counselor relationship?"

Jane didn't answer immediately. She sipped her champagne, carefully set the glass back on the table, and gave Elkins a long look. "What are you trying to find out?"

"Let me be blunt. Did he ever make a pass at you?"

"Yes."

"Was that the end of it?"

"No."

"Would you tell me about it?"

She picked up the glass and took another sip. "He asked me over for dinner one night. I don't know exactly how it happened. We probably had too much wine. We ended up in bed."

"You only had one encounter?"

"No, we had a brief affair, very bittersweet. I knew it was wrong for him, I knew it was wrong for me to ask him to continue. He was stronger than I was. He was able to break it off. I hope you won't talk about this. I wouldn't want to hurt him."

"When did this all happen?"

"Two years ago. My mother died in July. I started seeing him sometime after classes started in the fall. The affair was over by winter break."

"And you think that you might have recently mentioned Merchant to Father Bob?"

"I had coffee with him last week. We mostly talked about Bensen and Hendrickson. Since my mother died I've been," she paused, "that's not what I want to say. My father died when I was in high school, but I don't think that really registered. Since my mother died, I've really thought about death. And starting with Bensen's death, I've been obsessed with it. That's what I was talking with Father Bob about. I'm not sure I mentioned Merchant, but I may have."

"But you don't remember that, specifically."

"No, but I was pretty upset. I remember crying a lot. He makes me feel safe, I can let my feelings out." She looked at Elkins. "Even if I told him, that would be the end of it. He wouldn't tell anyone."

Elkins nodded in agreement. He didn't want to say anything, but tomorrow morning he was going to focus on learning more about Father Bob.

"We better get going. Stephanie is probably ready to serve. She says it's one of your favorites."

"What is it?"

"Can't tell you, it's Stephanie's surprise. I can tell you she has some excellent Stilton on the cheese board."

As they crossed the lawn, she slipped her arm through his. Even though the sun was setting, the air was still warm.

47

The next morning, Wednesday, Elkins and Pascoe arrived at the Interfaith Religion Center at 9:30 in the morning. They parked in the back and hurried through a light drizzle to the main entrance and took the stairway down to Father Bob's office at the back corner of the building. They stood at the closed door and looked at the schedule.

"Looks like he's not supposed to be in until 11:00," said Ray. After knocking, he tried the handle; the door was locked. They noted that across from his office was the entrance to the building's mechanical room. Pascoe unlocked the door of the mechanical room and ran her hand over the interior wall until she found the light switch. After Ray was in the room, she carefully closed the door behind them. The walls were covered with electrical panels, phone and cable boxes, controls for the heating and cooling system, and plumbing shut-off valves.

At the back of the room was a steel door. Pascoe slid a master key into the lock. Then, grasping the handle near the end with a folded handkerchief, she pulled the door open and they peered into the tunnel.

"Very convenient," said Pascoe. "Let me quickly dust these for prints. Maybe he wasn't as thorough at this end."

"Now if we just had a motive or some hard evidence," said Ray. "We can't ask for a search warrant just to do some fishing. Maybe we should look around his office."

Pascoe raised her eyebrows. "This doesn't sound quite kosher."

"Oh, but it is. As the acting head of campus security, I'm also the titular head of the fire department, the fire marshall, if you will. I'm just making a routine inspection of a campus-owned building to make sure there are no potential fire hazards."

"Well, I'm not sure that...," Pascoe's rebuttal was interrupted by the chirp of her phone. She listened for a long moment and turned to Ray, "There's been a shooting at the medical center, one of the staff psychiatrists."

"You get a name?"

"Margrave."

"Dead?"

"Not yet."

"Did they apprehend...."

"No, the assailant got away."

Pascoe double-parked in front of the Professional Arts Building, joining a long line of emergency vehicles. The corridor outside Margrave's office was blocked off, and Bill Baker, the head of security at the medical center was waiting for them.

"What do you know?" asked Pascoe.

"Not much. The security man at the staff entrance to this wing remembers Margrave arriving before 8:00. He says he commented to Margrave that he was the first one in."

"Any response," asked Pascoe.

"Just a greeting, nothing special that he remembers. This area doesn't really get busy until close to 9:00. That's when most of the clinics open."

"Who found Margrave?"

"The young women who delivers mail and records." Baker looked at his notes. "Her name is Amanda Bliss, said she had just pulled her cart off the elevator, this is the second office she stopped at. She said the door was ajar, and she saw Margrave on the floor."

"Did she see anyone in the hall or getting on the elevator?"

"Says she doesn't remember anyone specifically. I have her waiting at our office. I knew you would want to talk with her."

"How about Margrave?" asked Elkins

"Two shots to the chest. He was unconscious when he was found. He's in surgery. I don't think they're optimistic."

"Anything else?" Elkins asked.

"I have a short list of all the people who were in the area at the time. No one remembers seeing anything out of the ordinary. The receptionist in the clinic down the hall said she heard a couple of loud pops, but she didn't think anything about it. They're erecting steel for the new addition just beyond that wall," Baker pointed. "She just assumed the noise was from the construction."

Ray looked at the dark stain on the gray carpeting. The door to Margrave's inner office was ajar. He swung the door wider and went in; he was looking for an appointment book. Margrave's computer was on. Ray hit the space bar. The screen-saver, the medical center logo, disappeared.

Elkins looked at Pascoe. "He logged into his calendar. The first appointment was at 8:00 A.M."

"Who's the patient?"

"FB," he responded.

48

Father Bob was just coming out of the Interfaith Religious Center as Pascoe pulled into the circular drive next to the building. When he saw the police car, he ducked back into the door. Pascoe reached under her jacket, pulled out a 9mm automatic. "You call for backup," she ordered as she left the car. Ray phoned for help and followed her in.

The door of the mechanical room was just swinging shut as Pascoe reached the lower level. She unlocked the door and slowly swung it open. The lights were on, the room was empty, but the door into the tunnel stood open. She carefully approached the opening to the tunnel; in the distance she could see Father Bob moving from light to dark to light as he passed the evenly spaced bulbs. She cautiously pursued him, sprinting from one protected area to the next. Then he disappeared.

Pascoe assumed he must have reached the corner near the Engineering Building. As she peered from behind a cement pillar looking for the next area that would provide cover, Pascoe saw the muzzle flash and heard the bullet ricocheting off concrete walls as it passed her. She waited, looking and listening. No sound, no motion. She darted forward again, staying low and moving cautiously, scurrying from one protected area to the next. When she reached the point where the tunnel made a ninety-degree turn, she carefully looked around the corner, then dashed across the tunnel, using some equipment cabinets for cover.

Now she could see the figure again, this time at a greater distance. She pursued again, but suddenly he disappeared into the gloom. As she crouched in the darkness, she remembered the entrance to the carillon. She moved forward carefully, trying to find cover as she went.

She reached the alcove for the carillon entrance and searched the opening for any sign of movement. All she could hear was the sound of her breathing and the steady mechanical hum of distant equipment. She stepped back and jammed the barrel of her gun through the wire light cage, breaking the bulb. She slid into the alcove, her eyes adjusting to the darkness.

Pascoe holstered her gun and slowly climbed the steel rungs of the ladder. When her hands grasped the final rung, she peered through the open trap door and waited—no sound, no movement. She lifted her head through the opening; then she carefully pulled herself into the carillon, retrieving her gun.

She paused for a moment. She didn't have to go any farther. He was cornered. They could wait him out. There was no reason to pursue Father Bob. Then she thought about him standing with a gun above the diag, crowded with students. She cautiously started up the stairs. Pascoe was less than half way when she heard a shot, slightly muffled. No bullets ricocheted off the granite walls around her.

She stood for a long moment and waited, then slowly climbed toward the tower, gun at the ready, alert for any sudden movement above. Pascoe crept up the final few stairs. First she saw the bottoms of his shoes, heels on the floor, toes splayed at odd angles, then the legs, and finally the rest of the body. A pistol lay on the worn oak floor near Father Bob's head in an expanding pool of blood.

Pascoe stood there looking at the body. She heard Elkins climbing the stairs. He stood at her side for a long moment, breathing hard, and then he broke the silence. "We have the killer, now we need the motive."

49

Ray stood at the side of the hospital bed. "How are you feeling today?" he asked.

"Better, lots better. Today I feel like life might be worth living. For the last four or five days, I wasn't sure. I've really learned about pain. I now have an understanding of what soldiers go through."

"I've been by to see you a couple of times over the last week," said Elkins, "but you were sleeping. They've really kept you heavily sedated."

"Yes," said Margrave softly.

"I'd like to talk about what happened, if you feel strong enough. There's no rush. We can wait a few more days, if that would be better."

Margrave looked up at him. "I can tell you what I know, but I don't feel totally lucid."

Elkins placed a small recorder on the bedside table near Margrave. "You know that Father Bob killed himself?"

Margrave nodded, "Wife told me. Where?"

"The carillon."

"That fits."

"We've been able to piece together what happened, but we still don't know why. That's what you could help us with."

"Long answer or short answer?"

"Whatever you can do."

"Short answer. He knew, as a therapist, I was going to have to go to the police. I'm sorry I waited. This might have all been prevented." He paused, "Well, some of this might have been."

"What did you know about him?"

"Well, I didn't really know anything at first, but I finally put two and two together. I just didn't think it was possible. During our last session, I finally realized that his problems where a lot more extensive than I had thought. Would you hand me the water," Margrave gestured toward the tray at the side of the bed.

Ray picked up the container—stainless steel, a straw sticking through a hole in the cover—and passed it to him.

Margrave held the container carefully and drank from the straw, small sips, stopping to breathe between sips. Eventually, he handed it back.

"I've known Father Bob for a number of years. He's part of a university-wide group that meets for lunch once a month. The group includes people involved in counseling and therapy. I was impressed with him, smart, knowledgeable, verbal. A few months ago he contacted me, said he had some problems he needed help working out. He started seeing me twice a week. It took him a few sessions to tell me what was bothering him. Turns out he was sleeping with a number of the women he was working with."

"Working?"

"Working, as in counseling. Told me he'd never been very good at celibacy, but this wasn't just a sex thing. He was feeling a need to control them. Sex was the most powerful weapon. He told me there was a regular pattern. He would try to get a woman to fall for him, and as soon as he was sure he had her, he would drop her. I prodded him on the number of women. He told me he used to be involved with one woman at time, but in recent months he had two or three relationships going." Margrave paused to regain his breath. "You can see the obvious ethical dilemma for me. I pushed hard on why he was engaging in this behavior, a behavior that was unprofessional and a betrayal of trust. I hate to invoke one of the clichés of the trade, but we quickly got back to mother."

"Mother?"

"His mother. He was an only child and his mother left his father, left him as well, for another woman. This happened when he was eleven or twelve. He had little contact with his mother after that point. He was raised by a stern, protective father, who engendered in his son the anger and hatred he felt for his ex-wife. Bob was sent to a Catholic prep school and a Catholic university, and sometime late in his undergraduate career, he decided to enter the priesthood. He later got a Ph.D. in clinical psychology. And until all this started, by all appearances, he was quite effective."

"What triggered the change?"

"Dalton, Constance Dalton. She came to him for help. She had gotten involved in a liaison with one of her colleagues...."

"But I thought Dalton was in therapy with you."

"She was. She had been referred to me by Father Bob. He said her problems were beyond the scope of his counseling. Dalton was the catalyst that awakened all those feelings and all that anger he carried for his mother. You remember that it was an analogous situation. When Dalton started with him, she was considering leaving her husband and son for a woman. She was upset and confused. I guess after that he started to lose control. It took a number of months, but he became obsessed with getting the woman who, he felt, took Dalton away from her husband and son. It's a powerful bit of transference. All he knew about the other woman was that she was one of Dalton's colleagues, perhaps someone in the same specialty." He stopped and gestured toward the container of water.

Ray picked up the container. "This is almost empty, I'll have to get you some more." He carried it to the nursing station and returned with one filled with water and ice. Margrave passed it back to Ray after drinking.

"When did you learn about this?"

"He had an appointment on Monday. At the end of the session I think that he went further than he had intended to. When he came in on Wednesday I confronted him, asked him directly about his involvement in Benson's death. He told me everything. I think he had planned to kill me."

"So tell me about Bensen."

"He said that he had assumed that Bensen was her lover. He knew that Dalton spent time with her, and everything he knew about Bensen suggested that she was a lesbian."

"Did he tell you how he did it, how he got her to the carillon?"

"I asked. He said he set up a meeting with her in his office. Using the tunnels, he had purloined a small cylinder of nitrous oxide and a mask from the dental school. I don't know how he put her under, if he overpowered her or what. All he told me was that he put her out using nitrous and used the steam tunnels to get her to the carillon. He said he waited until some of her colleagues started coming out of the department meeting, then gave her a quick push through the window. Said her academic robes were the window-dressing. He gloated when he told me about it, said it was the perfect crime."

Elkins asked, "Did he tell you how he got the academic regalia?"

"Didn't elaborate, but I realize now how sociopathic and very manipulative he was. I'm sure he was able to get people to do almost anything he wanted them to."

"How about Hendrickson?"

"He said that after he killed Bensen, he became suspicious that perhaps Hendrickson was the object of Dalton's affections. He had seen them having coffee in the Union, and he sensed that they were intimate. Father Bob said that once he killed Bensen, the second one was easy. He said he hadn't really planned it, but when he saw her car at the Chesterton's it was all too easy. He had raced sports cars in college and knew all he had to do was cut some brake lines. Said he didn't know what effect it would have, and it turned out better than he hoped for."

"But why Arden?"

"He had committed two seemingly perfect crimes. He thought he could get away with another one. He knew Arden and Dalton were friends, perhaps more than just friends. Arden had told him some ex-con had threatened her, so he decided to take advantage of the opportunity. Said he couldn't believe that it didn't work. I asked how he felt about almost killing someone not involved. He said it happens in war, collateral damage."

"Dalton, we skipped her. Another nitrous oxide victim before the carbon monoxide?"

"He said Dalton did herself in. He was sorry, but it was probably for the best. Said it's hell growing up wondering about your mother, who she's with, if she ever loved you. Bob said Dalton's death would allow her son to get on with his life. He wished his mother had killed herself. At that point he pulled out a pistol and said something like, " Of course you appreciate why I have to do this.' That's about all I remember."

"It fills in all the pieces," said Ray. We will have to verify some of the physical evidence, but this ties it all together."

"You know," said Margrave, "I've done work in post-trauma therapy—policemen, firemen, rescue people. After you were shot at, I was going to offer to give you whatever assistance I could. If fact, you were on my call list the day...."

"I could still use it," said Elkins. "As soon as you've recovered."

"We'll probably have to bring in someone else. They can work with both of us," said Margrave with a weak smile. "We'll get a group discount."

50

Ray was standing in the kitchen when Jane pushed the screen door open and came in carrying a brown grocery bag. She set the bag on the counter and slid under Ray's arm and gave him a playful kiss on the cheek. "Stephanie sent you a gift. She said it was special."

"What is it?"

"You're going to have to look. It's not a surprise if I tell you."

Ray reached in the bag and pulled out a bottle of Krug. He looked at the bottle and said, "Wonderful."

"There's something more."

Ray looked in the bag again and pulled out a small can, frost forming on its exterior. "Stephanie is amazing; I don't know how she remembered this."

"What is it? Stephanie wouldn't tell me, and I couldn't read the label."

"It's concentrate, white peach concentrate. You mix it with champagne. It's very special. Get me a glass pitcher, will you. They're under that counter."

Arden opened the can and the champagne bottle, mixed the chilled champagne and peach juice, and filled two hollow-stemmed glasses. She handed one to Ray, lifted hers, and in a raspy voice said, "Here's looking at you, kid."

Ray responded, "Of all the gin joints."

She sipped, "This is superb. I imagine after you've given a woman a couple of glasses of this, you...."

"Feed her supper. Would you carry the shrimp out to the grill?"

They went out on the deck, and Ray opened the grill, adjusted the temperature, and carefully laid out the shrimp on the hot grate. He brushed them with marinade and turned them over. As he repeated the process several more times, Jane carried out the rice and salad, and set the table. Ray carried the plate of shrimp to the table.

"I'm impressed by your culinary skills," she said.

"It's something I enjoy."

As they started eating, Jane said, "I've been hearing bits and pieces, can you put the whole story together?"

"I can tell you what I know, and what I assume. Hopefully, we're close to the truth."

Arden gave him her wry smile, a smile he was starting to appreciate. "You're still struggling with some epistemological issues."

"Exactly," he said returning her smile and sharing her joke. He proceeded to tell her about Margrave's statement. Then he told her about finding the cylinder of nitrous oxide hidden in a closet in Father Bob's office. He also told her about the ballistics tests done at the state police labs that verified that the rifle found in Father Bob's trunk was the same one used in the shooting at her townhouse.

"There's one thing you will find especially interesting," he said as he wound down his story.

"What's that?"

"That rifle, the one he fired at you," he paused, "and me. We're both lucky. The fellow at the lab said the scope was way off. The weapon fired to the left. Either the scope wasn't sighted in properly, or it got banged on something. Anyway, we're lucky, both of us."

Jane filled their glasses again, and they sipped quietly, each lost in their own thoughts. Ray was looking at Jane. For the first time in months he was feeling relaxed, for the first time in several years he was feeling truly happy. The dark shroud that had been hanging over him was finally lifted. He was starting to think about the future.

CPSIA information can be obtained
at www.ICGtesting.com
Printed in the USA
LVHW091021030320
648714LV00002BA/356